CITY OF
GOLD

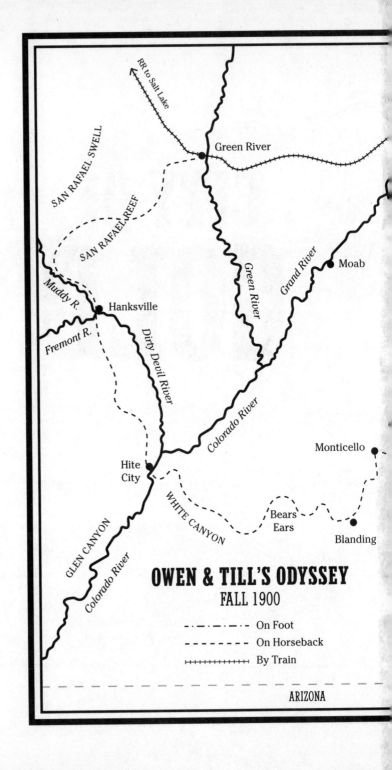

RR to Salt Lake

SAN RAFAEL SWELL

SAN RAFAEL REEF

Green River

Green River

Grand River

Moab

Muddy R.

Hanksville

Dirty Devil River

Fremont R.

Colorado River

Hite City

Monticello

WHITE CANYON

Bears Ears

Blanding

GLEN CANYON

Colorado River

OWEN & TILL'S ODYSSEY
FALL 1900

·—·—·—·—· On Foot

‑ ‑ ‑ ‑ ‑ ‑ On Horseback

⊦⊦⊦⊦⊦⊦⊦⊦ By Train

ARIZONA

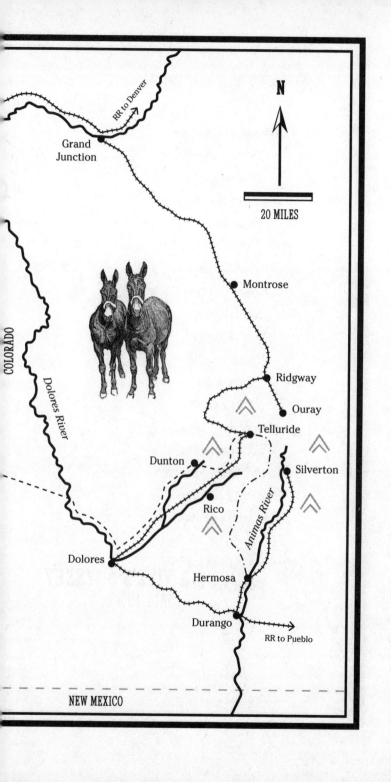

N

20 MILES

RR to Denver

Grand
Junction

Montrose

COLORADO

Dolores River

Ridgway

Ouray

Telluride

Dunton

Silverton

Rico

Animas River

Dolores

Hermosa

Durango

RR to Pueblo

NEW MEXICO

ALSO BY WILL HOBBS

Changes in Latitudes

Bearstone

Downriver

The Big Wander

Beardance

Kokopelli's Flute

Far North

Ghost Canoe

Beardream

River Thunder

Howling Hill

The Maze

Jason's Gold

Down the Yukon

Wild Man Island

Jackie's Wild Seattle

Leaving Protection

Crossing the Wire

Go Big or Go Home

Take Me to the River

Never Say Die

CITY OF
GOLD

WILL HOBBS

HARPER

An Imprint of HarperCollinsPublishers

Library of Congress Cataloging-in-Publication Data

Names: Hobbs, Will, author.
Title: City of gold / by Will Hobbs.
Description: First edition. | New York : Harper, an imprint of
  HarperCollinsPublishers, [2020] | Summary: "Determined to
  recover his family's mules, fifteen-year-old Owen is joined by
  his kid brother and Telluride's notorious marshal in pursuit of a
  rustler—all the way to Butch Cassidy's hideout"— Provided by
  publisher.
Identifiers: LCCN 2019033269 | ISBN 9780061708817 (hardcover)
Subjects: LCSH: Frontier and pioneer life—Colorado—Juvenile
  fiction. | CYAC: Frontier and pioneer life—Colorado—Fiction. |
  Robbers and outlaws—Fiction. | Mules—Fiction. | Single-parent
  families—Fiction. | Colorado—History—19th century—Fiction.
Classification: LCC PZ7.H6524 Cit 2020 | DDC [Fic]—dc23
LC record available at https://lccn.loc.gov/2019033269

ISBN 978-0-06-170881-7

Typography by Laura Mock

20 21 22 23 24 PC/LSCH 10 9 8 7 6 5 4 3 2 1

First Edition

to my brother Ed,
who kept asking after my mules

and to my nephew Matt,
remembering the best of times
in the wild San Juans

CITY OF
GOLD

1

IT'S YOUR MISFORTUNE

OUR MULES WERE whickering in the dead of night. Hercules and Peaches were in distress and trying to get my attention. Something was wrong but I wasn't able to do a thing about it. For some reason I couldn't even move. Their whinnies turned to squeals of terror. "Wake up, Owen," my father was saying. Pa was at my bedside, shaking my shoulder. "The barn's on fire."

Now that I'd scared myself awake, I found myself not in my bed back in Kansas, but on the kitchen floor of a two-room house in southwest Colorado. Moonlight was pouring through the kitchen windows. It took me a couple seconds to get my bearings. Pa was eight months dead. We were on our own now, my mother and kid brother and me. Ma was asleep in her room. Till was on the couch at the other end of our kitchen and sitting room, having a bad dream of his own. He was thrashing in his blanket like a wildcat caught in a grain sack.

Here came the whickering again, louder than would have been possible behind closed barn doors. Somehow our mules were out of their stalls and out of the barn. I peeled back my blanket, rose from my straw tick, and got dressed as quickly and quietly as possible.

I glanced toward Ma's door and back to Till. They hadn't roused. Best to look into this without waking them. Ma called me "the man of the house" though the expression was three sizes too big for me—I was a boy of fifteen. It meant she was counting on me. I reached for my mackinaw coat and felt hat on the pegs by the door and let myself outside.

All was quiet except the burbling of Hermosa Creek and the breeze in the pines. I looked toward the barn, lit bright by the moon, and saw the doors standing wide open. At least the barn wasn't on fire.

As I buttoned my coat against late September's keen night air, I heard a bit of clatter and looked in the other direction, toward the train tracks that ran from Durango to Silverton. I was stunned by what I saw, a rider in the moonlight heading out of our driveway and across the railroad tracks. He was turning north onto the wagon road.

The rider was trailing a packed horse and two

2

unloaded mules, the first as big a mule as you'll ever see, the second with spotted hindquarters. Hercules and Peaches without a doubt.

I was about to shout at the thief but stifled the impulse. Do something and fast, I told myself, and ran toward the barn.

At my pounding footsteps, our saddle horse whinnied nervously from her stall. "Queenie!" I called, and she nickered back. I had to calm her and feed her a handful of grain before she would take the bit. Once bridled, Queenie let me lead her into the moonlight and saddle her with no further objections.

I tried to get a fix on the time of night. That shiny full moon had most of its arc yet to travel. It was still in the east, above the ridge across the Animas River. Midnight, maybe? Come daylight the scoundrel would be long gone.

Follow him, and then what? I didn't have a thread of a plan. I only knew we'd be sunk without those mules.

I might be making a big mistake, but I had to take the risk. I fetched the lumber pencil I kept on the windowsill, grabbed a mill scrap, and wrote in capital letters:

THIEF STOLE OUR MULES—MIDNIGHT—
I'M HEADED NORTH ON QUEENIE

By the time I rode out of our place and took to the wagon road, the crook was out of sight. As I passed by the settlement of Hermosa there was nobody around, no lamp burning in the general store.

Crossing the bridge over Hermosa Creek, I was about to urge Queenie into a trot but held off as the Hermosa Creek Trail came to mind. In early August, a few weeks after our first day at the new place, I rode a couple miles up the creek trail. How far it went into the mountains I had no idea. Any chance the rider had taken the trail instead of sticking to the wagon road?

Silverton, if that's where he was heading, was forty miles up the road. On the road he'd be spotted for sure, any number of times. Wouldn't he try to get off it as soon as he could?

I went with my hunch and started up the trail. Before long I came to a stretch of soft dirt and puddled rainwater where I found what I was looking for—fresh tracks of mules as well as horses. A mule has a smaller hoof, and ours were unshod, as were these. Now was the time to pick up the pace, but under the trees the moonlight was scarce and the trail rocky. I had to bide my time.

My mind went to the why and wherefore behind the stealing. From our place we'd seen mule teams pulling freight up the road to Silverton, and unharnessed mules being driven that direction. They were indispensable to the mining towns and especially the mines, far better suited to the work than horses or burros and therefore of greater value. The gutter rat I was tracking had no doubt studied the excellence of our mules from the road, then waited on the full moon to do his dirty work. Remembering the squealing scream of terror I'd heard through my sleep, I wondered if he struck one of our mules. If so, I was hoping he was rewarded with a swift kick.

A couple hours up the trail, well past where I'd been before, I left the pines and entered a long meadow bathed in moonlight. The high peaks above the forest came into view, already showing snow in the last week of September. The meadow was sprinkled with cattle, some up and grazing in the moonlight. Rounding a bend in the creek, I made out a fire in front of the trees at the far end of the meadow. Who would have a blazing campfire going in the middle of the night?

Someone who'd recently arrived.

What was my next move?

Presume upon the better angels of his nature, I decided. If he had any.

As I neared the trees I saw one man and two horses. The man was sitting on a log close to the fire. His horses were tethered to nearby branches, not hobbled and not in the corral between him and the creek.

I couldn't make out his features as yet. His floppy hat was pulled low, but he was aware of my approach. How could he not be, as conspicuous as I was in bright moonlight on open ground? His black beard was cropped short.

I spotted a rifle in its scabbard on the riding horse. The canvas pannier bags off his packhorse were propped close at hand against the log.

"Evening," I said as I drew closer yet.

"Not hardly," he grunted.

I swung out of the saddle and walked a little closer, Queenie's reins in hand.

"Hold it right there," he barked. He appeared to have a wad of tobacco in the side of his mouth.

In the moment I noticed his gun belt I tried not to show my alarm. He had a big revolver on his hip, maybe a Colt .45.

A slab of meat in his frying pan was at hand, but he wouldn't have cooking coals anytime soon. Why such a hot fire? The night was cold, but not that cold. "Any luck hunting?" I asked. "Get an elk?"

"Just before dark, but what business is it of yours? Inviting yourself to supper?"

"I've never seen an elk. I'm new in the country."

"Not interested in your life story and not looking for company."

The man's cruel face and utter lack of civility were chilling, but I pressed on. "We're farmers. We left good ground behind in eastern Kansas, pulled up stakes in favor of southwest Colorado after my father died of

6

consumption."

"'It's your misfortune and none of my own."

"Both of my grandmothers died of it, too. Ma calls it the family curse. We're trying to make a new start where the air is dry and we won't catch it."

"State your business, kid."

He had some kind of metal rod propped on a rock. Its low end was in the fire.

"I won't keep you from your supper. The thing is, we're hanging on by the skin of our teeth. It cost us plenty to move our farm tools and animals out here, and the only way we can keep from going under is if we can sell crops next summer."

"So?"

"Our ground's never been plowed and our mules are missing."

He laughed. "So that's what this is about. You're wondering if I've seen your mules."

"I tracked them up this trail. Have you seen 'em?"

Here was his chance. It would be so easy for him to say something like *As a matter of fact I happened upon two stray mules. Got 'em tied up back in the trees.*

"Ain't seen 'em," he said. "What do they look like?"

"One's a great big gelding, dark brown, with white around his eyes and a white muzzle. The other's a gray female, has Appaloosa spots on her rump."

"I'll keep an eye out."

"Please, mister, my mother and little brother and me aren't going to make it without those mules."

"I already told you I'd keep an eye out. Unless you're insinuatin' I stole 'em. Is that what you just did?"

There was a chance this man was plumb innocent. He could be an elk hunter.

I had to take a chance. "Hercules!" I called, real loud.

Hercules knew it was me, and whinnied back.

"Peaches!" I cried, and she whinnied in return.

The rustler rose to his feet. He was of medium height, lean and wiry. The effort to rise had caused him to wince. Perhaps he'd been kicked by a mule.

"They're back in the timber," I said. "I'll just collect them and go."

"You sayin' I took 'em?"

"No sir, by no means. How were you to know they were there? Whoever took them is long gone."

He spat a stream of tobacco juice into the fire, and then he drew his pistol. "Get along, little dogie, or I'll leave your gut-shot carcass for the coyotes."

The way he said that last part, raising his voice as he leveled his gun at my heart, left little doubt. I saw it in his eyes. This was more than a threat. He was on the verge of pulling the trigger.

I had to say something, but what? "Sorry," I said. "No offense intended." I turned away quickly, hoping against hope he wouldn't shoot me in the back.

I mounted up, wondering if I was drawing my last

breath. I rode off slowly, trying not to show my fear, wondering all the while if he was reaching for his rifle. Those next couple minutes on that moonlit meadow took an eternity.

2

TELL US WHERE WE STAND

THE SUN WAS rising over the rim of our narrow river valley as I rode into Hermosa. I got a friendly wave from the old man sweeping the porch of his general store. No doubt Joe Buckland was wondering where I'd been, to be riding out of the mountains so early in the morning. What an encouraging welcome he'd given us that first day we stepped off the train. "To my mind, you've got the best forty acres of farming ground in the Animas Valley."

Maybe the storekeeper had seen the thief snooping around. Something he knew might help me get our mules back. I should talk with him, but Ma and Till came first. I was mulling over how they were going to react. Till would be thrilled out of his trousers at hearing that an outlaw drew a gun on me. It was a scene out of his page-worn "Blood and Thunders." As it was, Till was finding southwest Colorado in the first year of the new century disappointingly civilized, not the Wild West he'd been expecting. To hear him tell it, he was "disillusioned."

As to how Ma would take to hearing the way my mule chase ended—me looking into the barrel of a gun—I had no doubt. Our family had Quaker roots dating to William Penn's colony and all the way back to England, and Ma abhorred violence with a passion. If she thought there was any likelihood of me dying by the gun like my grand-fathers, I wouldn't get a second chance at recovering our animals. Arriving home, I'd better measure my words.

At the sight of our new farm, bordered on three sides by the narrow-gauge railroad, Hermosa Creek, and the Animas River, I felt a sharp pang at how much we stood to lose. From the beginning, I was smitten with our new ground on the lap of the San Juans, one of the highest and most rugged ranges in the Rocky Mountains. "No finer country," Uncle Jacob had written, and I felt the same way.

Till had been keeping a lookout. Little brother raised a dust cloud as he ran down the drive. For a nine-year-old he had an extremely heavy foot. I got off Queenie and closed the gate behind me.

"You didn't find our mules!" Till cried, all out of breath.

"On the contrary," I said, reminding myself to watch my step.

"You caught up with the varmint what took 'em?" Till had a literary bent, and his lingo borrowed heavily from dime novels and Huck Finn.

"I tried to play on his heartstrings," I replied, "but he didn't have any."

"Why didn't you just take Hercules and Peaches and go?"

"He had a gun on his hip and threatened to use it."

"He drew on you?"

"It didn't come to that."

Till's disappointment showed, but he was happy enough at discovering that Colorado still had gun-toting outlaws.

Ma was waiting for us on the house porch, her face lit with relief and questions. "Owen, while you see to Queenie, I'll whip up a quick breakfast. Then tell us where we stand."

Till was sour on waiting, but Ma was the one person he never kicked.

Over breakfast I told what happened, starting with my dream. Ma was dead sick at the telling even though she could plainly see I was in one piece. Till was so rapt he never once broke in.

"Owen," said Ma when I was done, "you were brave to do what you did. Maybe too brave. Your father spoke to you in your dream. Has that happened before?"

"Plenty of times."

"Same here. How about you, Till?"

Till wouldn't meet her eye. He nodded while staring at a pine knot on the floor. Till was five when Pa first coughed up blood. Pa's years of suffering took an especially heavy toll on him, young as he was.

"Your pa is still with us, boys. Starting over was never going to be easy. It looks bad right now, but if we stick together and take it one day at a time, everything will turn out okay. We'll get those mules back, I know we will."

Till wasn't so sure. "How? What are we gonna do about it?"

"We'll go find the marshal in Durango."

Midmorning we boarded the train for the eleven-mile trip into Durango. Southbound from Silverton, its steam locomotive was pulling two passenger coaches, a baggage and mail car, and four open cars full of sacked ore concentrates bound for the smelter across the river from Durango's depot.

The passengers were nearly all men, miners from Silverton dressed in their go-to-town clothes. A dozen or so got off two miles down the line, at Trimble Hot Springs. It had a fancy hotel and restaurant, but mainly people went there to soak in the mineral pools.

After a brief stop in Animas City, with Till champing at the bit, we pulled into Durango.

Durango sprang to life in 1881, when the Denver and

Rio Grande narrow-gauge railroad reached the Animas River in the distant southwest corner of Colorado. Fifty miles downstream of the mining mecca of Silverton, Durango's location was ideal, with abundant farm and ranchland nearby and high-quality coal to be mined barely out of town. By '82 the railroad reached Silverton, its original goal, nestled in the high San Juans.

I loved Durango except for the coal smoke that often got Ma coughing. The smelter, the trains, and the power plant that produced electricity all burned coal, not to mention the cookstoves and heating stoves of Durango's residents, upward of three thousand. The ridges and mesas flanking the town kept the smoke from escaping when the wind wasn't strong enough to chase it out.

As we got off at the depot I was brooding about our chances of staying afloat. Ma had a bank account in Durango, but would never let me in on how much we had in it. On the same day she started the bank account, she met with the lawyer who'd sent us Uncle Jacob's will. If she learned anything new from the lawyer, she wasn't telling.

Not that I would fault her. All three of us were keen to escape the pall of tuberculosis, and her boys had been sold on Colorado ever since Uncle Jacob's first letter singing its praises. Our timing, though, was awful. The spring of 1900 was a terrible time to have sold our farm, no matter how productive it had always been, with fertile ground and plentiful rainfall. Most of the country

14

was climbing out of the depression, but eastern Kansas was still suffering from the Panic of '93. Farmers like us were getting so little for the contents of our overflowing corncribs, we were burning corn for fuel instead of buying coal. How bad a shellacking we'd taken when Ma sold the farm, I could only guess.

As it turned out, we never talked with Durango's marshal. His clerk told us we should've gotten off the train one stop sooner, in Animas City. The location of the alleged crime—our place in Hermosa—was in the jurisdiction of La Plata County's sheriff. Rather than take the electric streetcar at a nickel apiece, we decided to hoof it. Animas City was only two miles up the river.

3

MUSTER A POSSE!

LUCKY FOR US, we didn't have to wait to talk to the county sheriff. Nonetheless, Till was clearly dismayed as he laid eyes on the lawman, and I knew why. The sheriff wasn't carrying a gun. Otherwise Bud Norton looked the part with his walrus mustache, ten-gallon hat, and riding boots. Ma had barely broached the theft of our mules when Norton broke in with "Heard of you folks."

Ma was displeased but the sheriff didn't notice. "You're from the vicinity of Lawrence, Kansas. Quakers, I heard tell."

"The Religious Society of Friends, yes."

"Lost your husband to consumption—is that correct?"

Ma nodded, adding nothing.

"I've seen you around town. A pretty sight I might add."

Ma had no patience for that sort of tomfoolery. Her eyes went steely but the sheriff was too full of himself to notice. "They say your husband's brother willed his Hermosa property to you. Some folks around here called him 'Lucky Jacob Hollowell.' As the story goes, he bought that ground with his winnings from a card game in Cripple Creek, I believe it was."

Till was about to say he was right about that, but a sharp glance from Ma kept his tongue holstered. Ma had made an uneasy peace with inheriting an acreage won by gambling.

Uncle Jacob had written us a letter about the card game. He cleared out of Cripple Creek the next day. He'd heard good things about the San Juan Mountains and how fertile the soil was in the Animas Valley up the river from Durango.

"He went to work in the mines in Silverton to save up the money to get his farm going," the sheriff continued. "Then he worked over the mountain in Telluride. Nobody called him lucky after he fell down the shaft in the Smuggler-Union Mine last winter."

Ma didn't flinch. "All we learned was, he died in a mining accident."

"Fell how far?" Till had to know.

The sheriff scratched his whiskers. "Nigh a thousand feet, I heard tell."

Till's eyes went big as he looked my way.

"About our mules," Ma said, and had me relate what happened.

The sheriff was attentive, I'll give him that much. When I was done he said, "We don't get much rustling these days."

I remembered about the metal rod in the fire and told him about it.

"That would be a running iron," the sheriff said. "It's got a small bend on the business end. Rustlers use it to change one brand into another. That corral you mentioned has got a chute where he could confine your animals and rebrand 'em."

I described what our mules looked like and gave him a sketch of our brand, adding that it was the Greek letter omega.

"Why omega?" asked the sheriff.

"It means 'the end,'" Till blurted. "Pa put it by their rear ends! It's a joke!"

After forcing a chuckle, Sheriff Norton grabbed a pencil and closed the open space at the bottom of the omega. "I'd wager your thief did this with his running iron—now it looks like a tall hat. Your pa shouldn't have chosen a brand so simple to alter."

I asked Norton where the Hermosa Trail went. "Clear

up Hermosa Creek," he said, "to where it heads at Bolam Pass. But after the first fifteen or twenty miles, there's a side trail goes over the hill to lower Cascade Creek and meets up with the wagon road to Silverton."

"You figure the rustler is headed to Silverton?"

"Most likely. There's enormous numbers of mules up there hauling supplies to the mines. They're tougher than horses, more hardy, eat less."

"Smarter," I added. "So, what can you do?"

When he hesitated, Till cried, "Muster a posse!"

The sheriff was amused. "Our citizens would be mighty rusty at that sort of thing and unlikely to sign up. I'll send a telegram to all the marshals and sheriffs in the mining towns and counties so they can be on the lookout."

"Horse and mule thievery is a hangin' offense," Till said darkly.

"Not in La Plata County. But when we catch him, he'll do jail time in the state pen."

Till wasn't done. "I know for a fact about an outlaw gettin' hung in Durango back in '81."

"That was a lynching, son, not a legal hanging. Durango was barely getting started. How'd you know about that, being so recently arrived?"

"Been askin' around," Till replied.

"Nineteen years ago Durango was sure enough wild and woolly. Two outfits of cattlemen from New Mexico were up here shooting it out. Some of 'em had been

19

shady characters in the Lincoln County War, ran with William Bonney, if you've heard of him."

Till jumped to his feet. "Billy the Kid! And Billy the Kid rode with the Stockton gang here in Durango."

"Wait a minute, where'd you get that?"

"From a book. Billy the Kid might still be alive."

"Don't believe everything you read in them 'Blood and Thunders.' Billy the Kid is moldering in the grave, same as Jesse James."

Till gave the sheriff a dirty look. "But not Bob Leroy Parker."

The sheriff seemed to be wondering how to extricate himself from this conversation. He shouldn't have gotten Till started.

Ma said, "Sit down, Till, that's quite enough. That is not what we came here for."

Till shot me a look. He didn't appreciate getting schooled by the sheriff. He was opposed to any sort of schooling, and getting cut off by Ma hurt his pride.

The visit was about over, but Ma had a few things to add. In parting she made sure the sheriff knew we were in dire straits without our mules.

"I'll sure let you know if I learn anything."

Ma looked unhappy, but she said, "We'd be much obliged."

As Norton saw us to the door, I noticed a glint in Till's eye, and realized what a perilous position the sheriff was in relative to Till's right foot. I stepped between them and we were out on the street, disappointed to put it mildly. As to the sheriff, he would never know how close he came to a royal shin kicking.

"Who's Bob Leroy Parker?" I asked Till a minute later.

"Butch Cassidy," he mumbled.

4

MONEYBAGS

IN THE DUMPS after seeing the sheriff, we waited at the depot in Animas City for our ride home. Ma was taking a stroll. Along came a kid slinging a bag of newspapers. He unfurled one and called, "Read all about it!" The headline shouted in big bold letters: ROOSEVELT IN COLORADO!

Till bolted from the bench and exchanged a nickel for news of his idol. WHISTLE STOP TOUR BEGINS IN PUEBLO announced the smaller headline beneath.

Theodore Roosevelt, the governor of New York and hero of the war in Cuba, was running for vice president.

"Just think, Owen, in July we were exactly where

Teddy Roosevelt is today! Pueblo is where you and me walked Peaches and Hercules in the yards before we switched to the narrow-gauge train. Pueblo is where we met Moneybags!"

I grimaced at the name. "Remember how friendly Moneybags was at first?"

"Oh, yeah, he really admirated H and P."

Till was always on the lookout for words to mangle. Ma had a theory he would outgrow it, but I had my doubts. You couldn't educate him any more than you could a snapping turtle.

"For a man in a three-piece suit," I went on, "Moneybags knew a lot about mules. He asked what kind of training they had. I told him they were a plow team, and mentioned we trained them for riding as well."

Till gave a snort. "That's when he said he'd been lookin' for a good ridin' mule. He was gonna pay two hundred dollars for Peaches! I suspicioned him of somepin'."

"You suspected him of something? Not that I remember. Like what?"

"He had a fish up his sleeve."

Our encounter with the stranger in Pueblo turned rapidly south after I declined his $200 offer for Peaches. When he suddenly announced he was willing to buy *both* our mules, we were dumbstruck.

The stranger reached inside his suit jacket for his wallet. Till looked at me as if to say, *What you gonna do now?*

"Really," I told the man, "they're not for sale."

"You can't mean that," he said, turning on the charm as he brought out four crisp hundred-dollar bills. They looked brand-new.

Though amazed, I wasn't tempted. "Our mother would say the same."

"It's more than twice what they're worth, take my word on it."

"Hercules and Peaches are members of the family," I explained.

Still he insisted, said there was a bank nearby, said he would pay in double eagles if gold suited me better than paper.

When I didn't respond, the rich man's demeanor turned dark and demanding. "You're wrong about your mother. She would say you're being foolish."

I thought about that but not for long. I took in the set of his square jaw, his piercing gray eyes, his dandy suit and derby hat, and I got my back up. "No thanks, mister," I said tersely. The stranger appeared to be a man in his prime, likely his early thirties, healthy and wealthy. What was his problem? Born with a silver spoon in his mouth?

He grabbed my wrist with an iron grip and said, "Look here, boy, I'm being reasonable."

"But not civil," I countered. He wasn't letting go.

It didn't end well. Till gave him a swift kick in the shin.

My right arm was free again, and we led our mules away. With a glance over my shoulder, I saw Moneybags standing there giving us a long and dirty look.

When we caught up with Ma, we gave her an abbreviated version of the encounter. She got the idea how angry the man had been, how devoid of sympathy. Ma remarked, "Some men have bile in their veins instead of blood."

In the here and now, Ma returned from her stroll. Along came our train, hauling mining equipment, hay, coal, groceries, lumber, mercantile goods, mail, and two coaches filled mostly with miners heading back to work in Silverton. We boarded and were lucky enough to find seats. We'd be home in fifteen minutes.

The rocking motion of a train would generally put Till to sleep, but not today. When he saw Ma reading the front-page story about Roosevelt, he lit up. "Listen, we could send T.R. a telegram about our perdicament. He would change his plans and commander a train to Durango. He'd get a posse together in a minute. Would we care if some reporters came along? Not if we got Hercules and Peaches back."

Ma had to agree with that, and said how unfortunate it was that we couldn't send a telegram out of Hermosa.

I derailed their conversation by whispering to Ma, "I should be there in Silverton when that skunk shows up."

Ma was considering my proposal, and I went on. "I could take the train to Silverton and check in with the town marshal. He'll need me to identify the thief and our mules."

"That may well be exactly what we should do," Ma allowed, "but we have to do this right. We're in a bad fix, Owen. We have to get them back."

"Don't I know it."

"Sheriff Norton didn't give us much thought. I'm not sure his say-so about Silverton is worth much."

As we got off at Hermosa, a hundred or more crates of fresh-picked apples waiting at the siding were being loaded aboard for Silverton. From a car up ahead, goods were being off-loaded to an old man with a team and wagon. A smile lit Ma's face. "There's the man we need to talk to." It was Joe Buckland, the grizzled old-timer who ran Hermosa's general store. Buckland had been a friend to my uncle and our indispensable adviser from the day we arrived.

Whenever I went to his store, I was riveted by Joe's stories from when the San Juan Mountains were part of the wild domain of the free-roaming Utes. During the Civil War, he was one of the first prospectors to cross the Continental Divide and discover silver and gold. The trickle of fortune seekers led to a full-on gold rush in the '70s, and the Utes were forced to sign away their lands rich in precious metals. When the mines began to be industrialized, Joe wasn't one of the lucky ones with a lode strike to sell to the companies. Rather than stay in the mountains and work for wages, he settled in

Hermosa. Confident the railroad would come, he opened a general store.

Ma and I pitched in to help the old man load his supplies onto his wagon. Till ran up the track to watch the steam engine take on water.

Soon as the train pulled out, Ma said to Buckland, "We need to see you in the worst way."

5

LEAVING IN THE MORNING

THE OLD-TIMER WAS standing on the porch of his store when Ma and I walked up a couple hours later. It was shaded by a pair of huge ponderosa pines. Joe Buckland nodded hello. "Where's Till?" he said with a grin.

"We left him to his own devices," Ma replied with a grin of her own. "He's either fishing for trout in the creek, gunning for prairie dogs with his squirrel gun, or panning for gold in the Animas."

"The boy's got it made. What brings you, missus?"

"Trouble."

"I gathered. Come in and set. I made some fresh coffee. Shouldn't be as vile as my usual fare."

Ma had me spool out my story. Buckland listened closely until I reported that Sheriff Norton told us our polecat was most likely going to sell our mules to the mines in Silverton.

"Why Silverton?" scoffed the old man.

Joe pulled out a map that showed all the trails and wagon roads, all the railroads and mining districts of the San Juan Mountains. He showed us the route to Silverton the sheriff had described, and then he pointed out half a dozen side trails and an abandoned wagon road where the stinker might leave the Hermosa Trail before he was halfway to Silverton. The graybeard's gnarled finger went north to the head of the San Miguel River. "My guess is, he's headed for Telluride."

"Why Telluride?" I asked.

"Telluride's bigger. Produces more gold than Silverton and employs more mules."

"He'd have to go clear over the mountains to get there, looks like."

"To my mind, a cunning thief would figure he'd less likely get caught if he made the longer trip to Telluride. Silverton's too obvious."

Ma had been listening closely. "Is there a train to Telluride that Owen could take?"

"Sure is, the Rio Grande Southern out of Durango. It reached Telluride in '91. But who's to say your thief isn't headed somewhere other than Silverton or Telluride? Maybe he intends to keep your mules for himself. Our sheriff's got horses and deputies, and should be tracking the rascal right this minute."

"Why isn't he, then," Ma insisted, "instead of sending telegrams?"

"Because he's lazy. Bud Norton didn't get my vote and never will. Between you and me, I wonder if those telegrams will even get sent."

"Tell me what you'd do if this happened to you, Joe."

The old man scratched at that beard, wild as tree moss. "I'd track him on horseback or on foot, if I was a younger man, that is. Any tracks are likely his, especially if they look fresh."

"How's that?"

"To begin with, folks don't use the trails much these days. They travel on the railroads and wagon roads. And here's another thing. The trails will be soft and muddy after all the rain we got last week. Most of the old tracks woulda gotten erased. The new ones—and there'd be plenty—would be from his horses and your mules."

"What if you lost the track?" I put in.

"I'd proceed to Telluride and see if I might catch sight of those mules. God helps them that helps themselves."

Ma and I went home in a quandary over where we stood, what we should do, and when we should do it. Ma was thinking of me picking up the rogue's trail where I encountered him and seeing if I could track him from there. "But slowly, lest you catch up with him before he gets wherever he's going." *Amen to that,* I thought. On

30

foot would be slower and safer, we agreed. We had Pa's old rucksack for my food and supplies.

At supper, we were less than eager to share our deliberations with Till. Instead, we gave him a brief rendition of our visit to the store. He listened closely, biting his lip. The kid was smart as a whip, and suspected we were holding out on him. Even so, when Ma extinguished one of the kerosene lamps at the usual stroke of nine, Till hit the sack and went to sleep in his habitual manner, like falling timber. By the light of the other lamp turned down low, Ma and I stayed up whispering at the kitchen table. We had a lot of figuring to do.

In the course of our back-and-forth, Ma admitted we were worse off than I knew. She finally told me about her meeting with the lawyer who sent us Uncle Jacob's will. He revealed that our new property wasn't free and clear like we thought. The lawyer had recently learned from the First National Bank that Uncle Jacob had been borrowing heavily against his acreage in Hermosa.

"What does that mean?" I asked her.

"Taking out loans to raise cash, to build the house and barn, and sink the well. Jacob never mentioned a whiff of this in his letters. By the time we inherited the property, the bank owned more than half of it, and they were planning on selling it."

I held my breath and asked, "So, what did you do?"

Ma's features took on a look of pride and defiance. "I paid off Jacob's loan. It took nearly all we had from the sale of our Kansas farm. Now we own our new place free and clear, which to your pa's way of thinking and mine is the only way a farmer can sleep at night."

"Let's say we get our mules back. How long can we manage without money coming in?"

"A year maybe? We'll have to live close to the bone."

It was like she'd hit me up the side of the head with an ax handle.

"We won't be able to start our apple orchard," Ma continued, "but there'll be a market for all the strawberries, potatoes, and other produce we can raise if we're able to plow in the spring. Everything depends on that."

"As for cash, we'll need to buy a headgate so we can let creek water into the ditches."

"We'll need to buy all sorts of things," she said soberly.

"Where does that leave us?"

Ma dispelled the tension with a smile. "I hear your father saying, 'Seize time by the forelock, it hath no hindlock.'"

With that, we decided to take old Joe's advice. We better not sit and wait for the law to recover our mules. I'd be leaving in the morning.

6

TRACKING THE SKUNK

SOMETHING IN MY rucksack was jabbing me in the back, but I wasn't attending to it. I was only a couple miles up the Hermosa Trail and trying to make time. I kept looking over my shoulder, half expecting to see Till.

My pack was heavy enough without the tinned fish and some other stuff I'd added at the Hermosa Store. Mostly what I stopped for was that map of the trails and wagon roads of the San Juan Mountains and some parting advice from Joe Buckland.

Till had made my leaving ugly. Most of his ruckus he directed at Ma, which was nothing new. I once heard Pa remark that Till came into the world feet first, fists clenched, and hollering at his mother. He woke earlier than usual, before dawn, to the sight of Ma and me tiptoeing around like church mice. I was gathering my things and Ma was lighting a fire in the cookstove. Somehow, during Till's sleep, he'd figured out that Ma was sending me on my own in search of Hercules and Peaches, and soon. It had taken no more than a creaking floorboard to rouse him. Till bolted upright and declared, "Owen and me can ride double on Queenie!"

"Owen's going on foot," Ma explained, trying to act unruffled. "Joe Buckland said it could be done, and I don't want Owen catching up to that man with the gun. We just need to figure out where he took Hercules and Peaches and let the law take it from there."

"Well, I'm going with Owen."

"No, you're not. You're staying with me. Sorry, Till, but you're too young for the mountains, and I need you here. I need your help."

"Like how?"

"For one, rigging Queenie to the buggy so we can get around."

Till said she didn't need his help, gave me a hard look, and went into a sulk. He knew I wasn't going to take his side.

"Till, don't forget," Ma said over breakfast, "you were going to 'radicate' the prairie dogs with your squirrel gun before they go down for the winter."

Mention of his .22 rifle, a gift from Pa, was meant to

soften Till some. "Don't care," he replied. He was biting that lower lip, never a good sign.

Ma pulled out the heavy artillery. "Well then, if you aren't going to make yourself useful like we talked about, you might as well start school tomorrow instead of after Christmas."

"They'll coop me up like a chicken!" Till wailed. With a bitter look in my direction, he shoved off from the breakfast table. When it came time for me to say good-bye, he was nowhere in sight. I hoped he was taking out his frustration on the prairie dogs. They were akin to the pestiferous ground squirrels on our Kansas farm and ten times as numerous. Their colony was smack on our best ground for growing crops.

I was maybe three miles up the trail and thinking Till had more sense than to chase after me. Whenever the locals talked about bears and mountain lions—we hadn't seen any as yet—he got very uneasy.

Minutes later, from behind me, I heard the sound of someone blowing like a horse galloped too long. I skittered into the forest and peeked from behind the trunk of an immense ponderosa.

Squirrel gun in hand, here came Till, his face wrought with a number of strong emotions. His clothes were wet from a fall in one of the creek crossings. I stifled the urge to call his name and let him run on by.

What was he thinking? He didn't have a pack and wasn't dressed for the mountains. It wasn't like I had an extra coat and bedroll for him.

Just as I was about to lose sight of Till, he came panting to a stop. He threw back his head and called, "O-wen! Ohh-wen! Ohhhh-wen!"

This wasn't easy. Little brother was ripping my guts out by the root.

A minute later, his breath collected, Till turned around and headed for home. I exhaled a sigh of relief. I was looking forward to being free of him for a change.

I figured I might as well repack. The culprit turned out to be the sharp corner of a book, *Behold the Dinosaur*. It was a gift from Pa, my squirrel gun in a manner of speaking. He was always encouraging my scientific bent, as he called it.

Noon by Pa's pocket watch, I was at the site of my encounter with the miscreant. I opened a tin of sardines as I sat on the log next to the ruins of his campfire. Back in the trees I found droppings where Hercules and Peaches had been tied. A nudge from my boot and I was looking at bits of the carrots I'd fed them from my own hand. I wondered what our mules must be thinking and hoped they weren't being mistreated. I swore I'd get revenge if they were.

As the trail climbed I left the ponderosas behind and entered the realm of aspen, fir, and spruce. A warm breeze was blowing golden leaves onto tracks of shod horses and unshod mules. Given all the muddy spots in the trail, they were easy enough to spot. I saw some older tracks but they were faint and few. The trail was seldom used, like Buckland had said. The peaks above me were painterly white with early snow against a sky "blue enough to knock you down," as my uncle had written. Here was a piece of luck at last, perfect fall weather as I hoofed it into his "shining mountains."

Eight or so miles up the trail, the prints of the outlaw's two horses and our two mules still obvious, I reached the intersection of the Hermosa Trail and the abandoned wagon road from Rockwood, a railroad stop on the way to Silverton. The wagon road was headed for Rico, a silver town gone bust on the headwaters of the Dolores River.

This had to be the road the old man talked about. Baby trees were taking it over, some knee-high. "Look careful," Buckland had said. "Your thief might've turned west up that old road. It goes over the shoulder of the La Plata Mountains to Rico. If that's what he did, he's likely headed to Telluride by way of Lizard Head Pass. If he continued north up the Hermosa Trail, you won't know whether it's Telluride or Silverton he's aiming for."

It was plain to see he hadn't taken the old wagon road. The tracks continued north on the Hermosa Trail. I came across droppings, "horse apples" as Till liked to call them, a day or two old.

"If you follow your rustler north into the high San Juans," Joe had added, "be careful once you leave the trees behind. That high up you got no cover, and the weather can get ugly in a hurry."

Six in the evening, footsore and weary, I camped at the edge of a meadow that flanked the creek. My spot had a little fire ring just back in the trees with a fine view of the meadow and the peaks above. I heated some stew and chewed on some jerky as the shadows grew long. The prolonged and eerie calling of an animal pierced the silence and sent a thrill through me. The bugle of an elk, I realized.

Darkness fell and the moon rose, still close to full. That elk sounded close. The bugling came every few minutes, such a strange love song. I wished they would come out of the woods.

I built up my campfire to keep the freezing night air at bay, and I fell to brooding. What was Ma thinking when she took most of what we made from selling the farm and paid off the Hermosa forty? Without even asking me if I saw my future in farming?

Back in Kansas I'd done what I had to do, but I wasn't looking forward to more of the same, even if I had accepted it as my lot. I was no man of the soil like my father, though he was much more than that. Pa reveled in all the new inventions and discoveries, and he encouraged me to "follow my curiosity into the twentieth century." That's why he was always giving me books.

Ma avoided any such encouragement. My eight years of schooling was behind me, and that was as much as most farm boys ever got. With Pa sick and unable, it was up to me to take the reins, and that's what I had done his last couple years. Farming was all Ma knew, and now more than ever our survival depended on it.

I added fuel to my campfire, and here it came—that sorrowful day we left home back in Kansas. I'd been blocking that memory, but now I couldn't stop it. Queenie was pulling the buggy and I was doing the driving. At the bend in the road where we were about to lose sight of the farm, Ma said, "Don't look back, boys."

Till didn't, but I looked over my shoulder, fighting tears, and my blurry vision burned a sentimental painting into my memory. The old Hollowell place was a model of what a farm should be.

From home it was seven miles into the town of Lawrence, Kansas, where Hercules and Peaches were waiting for us at the livery stable by the train yard. All the kit and caboodle we were taking with us, even the riding plow, had been loaded aboard boxcars the previous day. A couple miles short of town Ma told me to pull over by the cemetery gate. She said, "Let's stop and say goodbye to your father, boys."

On the buggy bench between us, Till recoiled like a slug showered with salt. He hated the cemetery, always stayed in the buggy. Till hadn't returned to the grave since that awful day we buried Pa.

"C'mon, son, it's your last chance."

"You said he wasn't there!"

"That's right, just his remains. He's in our hearts."

"So what's the point?" Till wailed.

Ma started crying, pulled out her handkerchief. "Please, Till, keep me and Owen company. This is a time for us to stand together."

We climbed out and made our way to the grave, Ma on my arm, Till walking behind.

The marker was in place, the mound had settled, and the sod had grown in thick and green. Till hung back but within earshot. The last time he'd been here, he was looking down on the coffin and wouldn't drop the clod of black dirt from his hand.

"Aaron," Ma began. "It's Mary and your boys. We're off to a new adventure. Your brother died and left us his forty in Colorado. Remember him waxing poetic about the rich volcanic soils? How good the market for produce was if only he could get to growing it? Wish us luck, darling. You'd be so proud of your boys. They're going to flourish in that dry mountain air, grow up healthy and strong. I know you're happy about that, with us safe. Don't fret, we're taking Hercules and Peaches along for the heavy pulling. You'll always be with us until the time when there are no more days."

Fighting my tears was useless. "Help me out, Owen," Ma said. "Say something."

"Pa," I managed. "Don't worry about us. We're going to do fine in the mountains. I'll help Ma and watch out for Till the best I can. We miss you something awful."

Behind me Till was sobbing. He was much too young

for all of this.

To my surprise I found him stepping to my side. "Pa," he said, "I'm gonna take my squirrel gun!"

Ma brightened with a smile. "We've got a train to catch, boys."

The bugling of the elk brought me back to the present. Lost in my sorrowful reverie, I hadn't noticed them gathering on the meadow right in front of me. Much bigger than deer, all bathed in moonlight, they were something to see—two dozen or so cows with their calves and one huge bull with a mighty rack of branching antlers.

7

TOO LATE TO TURN BACK NOW

NO MATTER MY bedroll and coat, sleep wouldn't come on the cold, hard ground. Finally I couldn't take it any longer. The moon had risen; by Pa's watch it was two in the morning. I crawled out from under the tarp, got my fire going again, and warmed up. I felt puny, plumb alone, and scared. After an hour by the fire, I tried to sleep but failed all over again. I couldn't quiet my mind for thinking what Hercules and Peaches were going through, what cruelties awaited them.

At last, first light. I had something to eat and took off hiking with a vengeance. The tracks of horses and mules were still obvious in the soft, wet ground. By midafternoon, with Hermosa Peak over my left shoulder, I reached the headwaters of Hermosa Creek. Every bit of climbing in that thin air had me gasping for breath. I huffed my way above the tree line and onto the alpine tundra, golden brown after weeks of heavy frost. Bolam Pass was in my sights. As I approached the pass, more and more peaks to the north raised their jagged, snowy heads.

Approaching Bolam Pass and looking for a fork in the trail, I had my map out. I was hoping the outlaw went west there, down through the forest to the Dolores River upstream of Rico. In that case, Telluride was his likely destination, by way of Lizard Head Pass. If he steered north, I would have to follow him into the treeless heights of the San Juan Mountains, presumably to Silverton.

My luck being what it was, the stinker's trail led north from Bolam Pass into the high San Juans. The map said RICO-SILVERTON WAGON ROAD, but that left me scratching my head. If ever it was a road, time and the elements had rubbed most of it out. A remote trail was what it had become, all the more attractive to a criminal making himself scarce. Horse apples on the tundra, not that old, told me I was still on his track. It looked like he was headed for Silverton.

Passing under Sliderock Ridge, I managed in the last of the daylight to reach a bit of cover under a cluster of stunted spruce trees. No stars appeared. I knew enough to figure that a cloudy night didn't bode well for the next few days. I slept in fits out of pure exhaustion.

Day three of my trek dawned cloudy gray with the wind picking up. The nice weather was done and gone. Encircled by mountain peaks, the route stayed amazingly high, where my lungs couldn't get enough air, where trees couldn't grow. The trail flanked Grizzly Peak and Rolling Mountain and finally, with the wind roaring, dropped into the headwaters of South Mineral Creek.

I spent the night in a spruce thicket that provided firewood and a windbreak. I put Pa's hatchet to use and made a bed of spruce tips.

When I set out in the morning of day four, I figured I'd be in Silverton in a couple of hours and talking to the marshal there. But when I reached the main flow of Mineral Creek and waded it, the tracks weren't headed downstream toward Silverton. The skunk had gone upstream, toward Red Mountain Pass.

I took out my map. The mining towns of Silverton, Telluride, and Ouray lay in a triangle with legs of fifteen to twenty miles as the crow flies, but each was separated from the others by indescribably rugged mountains. Our devious rustler had made it look like he was heading for Silverton, but that was a ruse. It might be Telluride, like Joe Buckland had guessed, but it might even be Ouray.

The tracks joined the wagon road alongside the bed of the spur railroad out of Silverton. This route had seen quite a bit of recent use, deep wagon ruts and all, and I couldn't tell the tracks of the scoundrel's animals and ours from all the others. The clouds were beginning to spit snow. I thought about Silverton and heated buildings. If I turned around, I'd be there in a few hours, safely checked into a hotel. What then, if it snowed all night?

After all I'd been through, I couldn't give in. I kept climbing as the clouds dropped and shrouded the peaks.

High on the mountain I came across deserted shacks and tailings and tunnels into the iron-red slopes, but no miners, nobody to tell me, "He went thataway." I didn't know it at the time, but the mining flurry on Red Mountain was history.

Up on the pass, next to some rusted machinery, I came across a marker: RED MOUNTAIN PASS 11,018 FEET ABOVE SEA LEVEL.

At the sign, the tracks of a small number of mules and horses left the wagon road onto an unmarked trail heading west. My map showed a trail west to Telluride from where I stood.

If I stayed on the wagon road, I would end up in Ouray.

I couldn't be sure that the horses and mules that left the road here were the outlaw's and ours. It seemed likely, though, in which case Joe Buckland was right after all. The thief was aiming to sell Hercules and Peaches in Telluride.

Our graybeard's last shouted advice came to mind. "Whatever you do, don't get caught up high in the weather!"

I didn't think long or well. Underneath, it was fear

that drove me, the looming ruin of our hopes and dreams. The wind blew wild and cold, I had a nosebleed, and my feet were freezing. I flipped up the collar of my mackinaw and plunged ahead as flakes big as quarters began to fall. An hour or more later, gasping for breath, I wiped the snow off a leaning trail sign that said BLACK BEAR PASS 12,840 FEET. In the clouds, I couldn't see farther than I might've thrown a rock.

This is crazy, I thought as I started down the other side. I was able to keep to the trail a couple more miles but lost it descending another slope. The snow came in gusts, heavy and wet. I took to sliding down the slick mountainside on my hindquarters. When I paused to rest, movement caught my eye. Below me, half a dozen bighorn sheep were moving from right to left and abruptly out of sight.

Before long my descent became almost impossibly steep. Heavy as the snow was coming down, I had no chance of spotting the trail. On the verge of falling into the abyss, I came across fresh tracks of the wild sheep. Their tracks led onto a narrow ledge. *Too late to turn back now*, I thought, and I started across the cliff. *Good thing Till isn't along.*

Shivering and shaking, I walked the slippery ledge one cautious step at a time. No more than half a hundred yards away, like an apparition in the cloud, the sheep appeared. They were huddled on a steep slope, standing on the switchbacks of the trail I had lost.

My ledge was heading for a dark cleft in the cliff. I had no idea what to expect there, and was shocked when the ledge came to a sudden end at a nearly vertical chute that ran down from above. I read the tracks in the snow. The sheep had jumped the chute to a ledge maybe six feet away and a foot lower than the one I was standing on.

On first glance I thought I could make the jump. I also knew I was more than half frozen and not in my right mind. A fall would be the end of me, but I had to get off of this mountain and soon.

I studied it out and decided it could be done with a bit of a running start. A grim laugh seemed to help. I ran to the edge and took my leap. My feet found the landing but couldn't hold. My hands reached out to break my fall, but my chest met the ledge with such force, the wind was knocked out of me.

It took a scary while before I was breathing again. I got to my feet with only scrapes. Five minutes later I was off the ledge and standing on the mountainside where the sheep had watched my antics. I was on the trail again but the switchbacks were disappearing by the moment under heavy snow. I thought I heard a steam whistle blow, and chalked it up to a delusion.

Farther down the mountain the snow changed to sleet and then to rain. I was able to make out where I was going. Grabbing hold of scrub willows and rocky outcrops, I worked my way down a creek that fell in leaps and bounds from the heights.

Mine works promised people and warmth, but I found them cold as the tomb. I headed down the steepening slope in the cloud, then held up, and it's a good thing I did. Yards away, at the brink of a precipice, the creek went over a cliff.

A few steps closer to the waterfall and I heard a whistle blow two, three times. I drank from my canteen, wishing the water were warm. The sun broke through, illuminating the scene below, a box canyon of stupendous proportions. Way down on the valley floor, a train was in motion. Chuffing and puffing and spouting smoke, its locomotive was pulling freight on flatcars.

My eyes went where the train was headed. Nestled in that alpine valley, hemmed in on three sides by soaring mountains, lay a mining town. This frozen fool was going to make it. Telluride was in my sights.

8

CITY OF GOLD

THE STORM CLOUDS were racing away as I planted my feet on the valley floor, where a heavy rain had fallen. Mud puddles were everywhere. Within minutes, at the closed end of the box canyon, I came across a mill complex with stacks belching black smoke. The noise was deafening. The industrial thunder, ominous and repetitive, was coming from rows upon rows of ore-crushing machines stamping up and down. Amid the din, workers were swarming like ants stirred with a stick.

Rocks clattering down chutes into the mills made a racket of their own. The ore was carried down the mountain in buckets suspended from two separate aerial tramways. The air was acrid with chemicals. I lurched on by, barely noticing the cyanide ponds if at all. I was still cold to the bone and shuddering. At a railroad siding, men in overalls were loading sacks of concentrates onto a flatcar. I failed to notice the boarding houses, store, and post office, and didn't realize this was something of a settlement. As I would come to learn, the place was called Pandora.

The road under my feet had deep wagon ruts and tracks of horses and mules. I had to hope that Hercules and Peaches were here, not who-knows-where. I intended to find them and soon. Somehow, some way, I would claim them for my own.

With a couple open miles to go, Telluride was in my reach at last. The edge of town looked like a jumble of ramshackle shanties thrown up cheek by jowl on the sloping floor of the towering box canyon. Till would've approved of the raw look of it, I thought with a grin.

Unbeknownst to me, the creek on my left was the fresh-born San Miguel River. Below Pandora it ran yellow with the residues of heavy metals hewn from the innards of the mountains.

Where the railroad spur and the stream steered toward the low side of town, the road aimed straight ahead and became Colorado Avenue, Telluride's main street. I was walking into the sun and no longer shivering.

In the first few blocks, the saloons outnumbered the stores, offices, and shops. I was thankful for the boardwalks. They kept me out of the muck and mire of the street, which was swarming with bugs. I was bitten by a horsefly while my attention was on six mules pulling a heavily laden freight wagon.

The men heading into the saloons looked rough enough to suit Till, and some were armed.

A few blocks farther on, Telluride looked substantial and prosperous. A banner strung across the street proclaimed the town motto, CITY OF GOLD. The courthouse and the New Sheridan Hotel were both faced with brick. The hotel included a restaurant, bar, and opera house.

Looking to get free of my rucksack, I considered a room for the night at the New Sheridan, but not for long. Ma had given me ten silver dollars for the trip and I had to watch every penny. A boarding house would be more like it. At the corner I walked up Oak Street in hopes of spotting one. A most unusual sight brought a smile. At the head of the street dozens of mules were returning single file to town with empty packsacks and no packer minding them. They weren't connected in a string; their halter ropes were looped around the forks of their pack-saddles. Each mule was free to go where it pleased, but evidently they were all making a beeline for the barn.

The street was lined with dandy two-story homes with all the frills of the Queen Anne style my mother admired along Durango's Third Avenue. Ma would have been tickled by the sight of these mules with empty pack bags, their working day done, promenading down this lovely street unaccompanied. The steep, sunny slope behind them was ablaze with aspens in their autumn finery. As if that display wasn't sufficiently colorful, a parade of red cliffs ran through those immense swaths of gold. My mouth was agape as the mules began to pass me by.

Intending to follow them to their stables, I ran to catch up. I was approaching Colorado Avenue when two men crossing the street caught my attention. The one with the gun belt looked an awful lot like our thief—the mackinaw coat, the hat, the short-cropped black beard.

As I reached the corner, the two men disappeared into the Sheridan Bar.

I couldn't be sure he was the one. There could be hundreds in this town who resembled him. What was I going to do, accuse him in the saloon?

Then what? Better to find our mules first. Then I could sic the law on him.

Here came some mule trains bearing heavy loads. Each string of sixteen was led by a man on horseback. The packers looked unsavory and unfriendly. The burdens their mules carried were familiar: sacked concentrates identical to the ones that passed our Hermosa place every day, heaped on flatcars and headed for the smelter in Durango. I'd heard it said that each sack weighed a hundred pounds. The mules I was looking at carried three—one in each canvas pannier bag and one atop.

I followed the mule parade across Colorado Avenue and downhill toward the railroad and the river. Where the packers led their strings to a flatcar on a siding, I headed west with the unburdened mules that were on their own and presumably heading for the barn. I would've followed them but was waylaid by my hunger. MARIE'S BAKERY said a sign on the corner across from the depot. I should celebrate my survival; something sweet would hit the spot.

That late in the afternoon I was lucky to find the store open. The shelves were all but bare, and no one was there except the raven-haired girl behind the counter. Her dress was colorful and painfully clean. I ran my grubby hands through my filthy hair in an attempt to tame it a little. "Good afternoon," she said with a wry smile. "How may I help you?"

I must've looked like a boulder with legs that tumbled off the mountain in the storm, gathering another layer of mud with every revolution. I met her eyes with a passing glance; she was so pretty I had to look away. I spied two long, skinny loaves of bread on an otherwise empty shelf and asked her how much for both.

"A nickel," she said brightly.

"You sure? Looks like supper and dessert to me."

"They're going stale. A nickel is fine."

I swung my pack off my back and began to open it up. Flakes of mud were falling to the floor. "No need," she said. "Come back Monday with that nickel."

"Monday?"

"Tomorrow's Sunday. We'll be closed."

"I lost track. I'll see you Monday, then."

I took the loaves from her hands and was about to leave, happy my embarrassment couldn't show through the sediment on my face. I had my hand on the doorknob. "You hiked into town?" she asked.

I let go the door. "Over the mountains from Durango."

"All that way . . . It's beautiful here, especially with the aspens turning. Is that why you came? Sometimes tourists come on the train and rent horses."

"A rustler stole our mules. I tracked them here."

"Really? What a story. We had a bank robbery here— the San Miguel Valley Bank—but that was eleven years ago. You've probably heard of it."

"I don't think so."

"Butch Cassidy and two cohorts. They stole twenty-one thousand dollars in greenbacks and gold coins. Some say it was more like twenty-four thousand. It was his first heist."

"My kid brother would know all about it. He loves those stories—men on horses, men with guns."

Our conversation was about to die out, but I kept it going. "About the mules coming off the mountain . . . Do the ones with nothing to carry come back to town on their own?"

"They do. They're free as birds. They might snatch at wildflowers on the way down, but mainly they've got hay and oats on their minds, back at the stables."

"The mules carrying loads need minding, I take it?"

"Uphill or downhill, they always have packers with them. Heavy labor is not their idea of a good time."

Just then I heard footsteps on the stairs. I glimpsed a woman—her mother? "I should be going," I said.

"Good luck finding your animals!"

Outside, while gnawing on the French bread, I eyeballed a string of packed mules passing by. About the diameter of my wrist, the bread sure was crunchy. I could save the second loaf for a club in case I got jumped in an alley. Now that I chawed on it some, I found the inside soft and delicious.

Too bad I hadn't learned her name, but there would be another day. I should have asked where the telegraph office was. I'd promised Ma I would send a telegram soon as I could.

I followed some unattended mules west onto Pacific Avenue past warehouses, saloons, boarding houses, a laundry, and an ironworks. Nearing the edge of town I saw the heads of a couple hogs bobbing down the river. No bodies, just the heads. I'd never seen a place half as raw as Telluride.

9

SOLD TO THE TOMBOY

ROGERS BROTHERS LIVERY & Feed was a big outfit. They had an office where you could rent horses, but I went around the side where the mules returning from the mines were headed.

I got as far as a corral where handlers were relieving mules of their pannier bags and packsaddles. I noticed a couple with running sores, which pained me greatly. A few others had swollen forelegs and ankles, most likely from being worked beyond their legendary strength and endurance. A mule's height and muscle strength come from its horse mother, while its leaner build and nimble legs come from its donkey father. The hooves and legs of a mule are stronger than those of a horse, which is why mules seldom go lame. Some of these were due for a good rest.

I asked after the head stableman and was pointed to a lanky fellow with a big silver belt buckle. I was afraid he'd throw me out on my ear soon as he heard what I was after. "Chet Hamlin," he said as he shook my hand.

I spit out my name and my problem. It wasn't half a minute before Hamlin was nodding, and broke in helpfully. "A stranger showed up with two mules day before yesterday. One was the biggest I've ever seen, and I've seen a lot of mules in my day. Wonderful animal in every regard. Dark brown with rings around his eyes and a white muzzle."

"That's our Hercules."

"An apt name, if he's yours. Stolen, you say?"

"From our barn in Hermosa. We brought him and Peaches all the way from Kansas to plow our new farm. Did you notice the brand? Did some of it look fresh burned?"

Hamlin was taken aback. "Didn't see a brand. The mule had been in some mud, come to think of it. They like a good wallow."

"Were you looking to buy them?"

"We would've bought both, but the fellow was only selling the big 'un and his packhorse."

"Was he a hard-looking man with a dark beard, short cropped?"

The stableman nodded, but cut himself short. "I stay out of police business. I've got my own concern to look after."

I didn't know what to make of that. "You were looking to buy Hercules, you said, but you didn't?"

"The buyer for the Tomboy Mine was keen on the big mule, and our pockets aren't as deep as theirs. The Tomboy is a big company."

"So, where would I find Hercules?"

"Might be still in town . . . could be up at the Tomboy."

"Where's that?"

"At timberline in the Savage Basin, six miles out of town and three thousand feet up. They rent big numbers of our mules for the daily trip up and down, but they own a couple dozen. Keep most of them up there year-round."

"What for?"

"To work inside the mountain, pulling ore cars."

The very idea was horrifying. I had to find Hercules and fast, while he was above ground.

"What about Peaches?" I asked. "She's gray, with spots on her rump."

"The man said he was keeping her for a riding mule."

"I better see the marshal here, and soon."

Hamlin's features clouded. "I wouldn't rush that. Do you have papers on the animals?"

"I'm afraid not."

"Better get the lay of the land first. You don't want to get on the wrong side of Jim Clark. He's a difficult man."

"Well, I'll be back, to rent a horse to go up to the Tom-boy."

"Good thinking."

The stableman asked if I had people in town. I told him I used to, that my uncle died in an accident in the Smuggler-Union Mine.

"Sorry to hear that. No doubt he was a union man."

"For certain. He sang its praises in his letters."

Chet Hamlin told me of a boarding house favored by men who had worked in the mines and were no longer able. I would be well received there. "Hurry along, you might catch supper. If I'm not mistaken, on Saturday it's beefsteaks and beer."

Oma Oleson's Boarding House was in the warehouse district not far from the depot and the bakery. Nobody was at the desk in the front parlor. I was surprised by the electric lights but shouldn't have been. Durango had electricity, same as Lawrence. Our new farm in Hermosa didn't, same as the old one in Kansas.

From down the hall came voices and the rattle of dishware. I tucked my unsightly rucksack behind the desk and made my way down the hall in hopes of a meal and a bed.

The doors of the brightly lit dining room were wide open. I spied three tables with grizzled men on benches shoveling food from platters and pouring beer from pitchers. There didn't seem to be a spot where I might squeeze in.

Heads and eyes turned my way, and the clamor of conversation was replaced by near silence. They seemed like they were looking at some rare curiosity. Two women bearing platters of beefsteaks stopped in their tracks. I must've looked like I'd been dragged through a knothole and beat with a stick.

I spoke up. "Sorry about the interruption. I was hoping to stay here. My uncle was a miner at the Smuggler-Union."

"What was his name, sonny?" called one of them.

"Jacob Hollowell."

Murmurs filled the room. I wondered if somehow my uncle's reputation was south of shady.

One of the men rose, steadying himself on the table. "Jacob Hollowell was my particular friend," he declared. His voice was raspy, his breath wheezing. "You must be his nephew Owen, from Kansas."

I was more than surprised. "That's me," I agreed. "Owen Hollowell."

"How 'bout that!" cried another man. "You're mighty welcome here. We got a bunk for the boy, Oma?"

The older of the two women, with a red-and-white-checked apron and her silver hair in a bun, was quick to reply. "You betcha ve do!"

Cheers filled the room.

My uncle's friend was beckoning, and a place opened next to him.

Seconds later they were raising glasses to the

memory of my uncle and to Local 63. Their accents were many. The wheezing ex-miner at my elbow, Merlin Custard, introduced himself as a "hard-rock Cornishman." I didn't know Cornishmen from corned beef, but his accent sounded English. He cleared up my confusion by adding that Cornwall was a region of England.

Merlin might have been no older than fifty but looked emaciated, spectral even. His nearly translucent skin, drawn tightly over the bones of his face, had a blue tinge. He stared at me with unblinking pale blue eyes and said, "You favor Jacob to be sure." As Merlin explained, he bunked next to my uncle when both of them lived and worked up at the mine, the Smuggler-Union. The men at supper had worked at half a dozen different mines, but they all knew Jacob because he was one of the leaders of Local 63, their union.

In no time at all I was looking at a steak, a baked potato, string beans and carrots, and a thick slice of bread. "Hope you're hungry," Merlin said.

"Starving."

"Dig in, then!"

I did as I was told. Soon as I slowed down, the men at the table wanted to hear my story. I explained that shortly after my father died, we learned we had inherited the Hermosa place from his brother who died in an accident in the Smuggler-Union. Their reaction at hearing that last part confused me no end. Some were muttering, others were exchanging wrathful glances. "What is it?" I asked Merlin.

"Your uncle was vice president of our union chapter. What did you—" Merlin ran out of breath but began again. "What did you hear of this so-called accident?"

"Only that he fell down a shaft."

"Fell?" Merlin was incredulous. A chorus of oaths arose.

Merlin fixed me with blue eyes blazing. "We believe he was pushed."

With that my uncle's friend clammed up, seized his knife and fork, and attacked his steak with a vengeance. I did the same, hoping I would learn more when the time was right.

As it turned out, the bed Ma Oleson had in mind for me was upstairs, where most of the two-dozen residents slept. Double bunks lined both walls; wardrobes for each man's clothes and possessions stood back-to-back in the middle of the room with passage around both ends.

Merlin pulled a sleeping sack off an upper bunk. "We'll have to empty his wardrobe, too."

"Whose?"

"Elias Eriksson, a Swede."

"Is he coming back for his things?"

"Not likely." Merlin had a wry gleam in his eye.

"Left town in a hurry?" I joked. "Law on his heels?"

"Nothing like that. He'd been doing poorly for some time."

"Hmm . . ." I said. "How long ago did he—"

"Expire? Just this morning. That's why his stuff is still here."

Sleeping in a dead man's bunk gave me the willies, but darkness had fallen and I had no alternatives. It took us several trips to carry the man's effects in our arms two flights down to the basement, where we left them in an empty steamer trunk. After the first load, Merlin was wheezing something awful on the stairs. I tried to talk him into letting me finish the job, but he wouldn't have it.

After that I took advantage of the opportunity to draw a warm bath and nearly fell asleep in the tub. I climbed the end ladder to that upper bunk, slipped into my bedroll, and lay my head on the pillow. I might have fallen asleep straightaway had I not paused to consider whose pillowcase this was. My next thought was to wonder after the Swede's cause of death.

With dread rising nearly to panic, I yanked the pillowcase off the pillow and tucked it under my bedroll. Ma had been extremely careful during Pa's illness to make sure Till and I stayed clear of his linens and such. All the while Pa was careful to cough into his handkerchief.

Eyes closed, I listened to the men arriving from downstairs. They talked a bit as they took to their bunks. I was so possessed by fear, I didn't register on a thing they were saying. After midnight by Pa's watch, I was still awake and listening to the ragged breathing of the sleeping men, like hacksaws ripping metal. It sounded as if I had landed in a hospital ward.

I lay there trying not to take the stale and sickly air into my lungs. Finally I couldn't stand it any longer and crept down the stairs to the front parlor, bedroll under my arm.

Merlin was down there reading a book, Stevenson's *Kidnapped*. As I sat in an easy chair close by, his unruly, arching eyebrows asked a silent question. "Couldn't sleep," I said.

"Not surprised. We make a fearsome racket. Were you concerned?"

"Somewhat," I said. I wasn't going to say the word *tuberculosis*.

"It's not TB, Owen. What I've got—most of us here— is silicosis, also known as 'miners' consumption.' It's the result of the rock dust we took into our lungs from the compressed air drills we used in the mines. 'Widowmakers' they were called, for good reason. Just lately 'wet drills' took their place. The new drills have a hollow center. Water under pressure shoots through the tip of the bit and keeps the rock dust down. Our days are numbered, but don't worry, you can't catch what we've got."

10

IS THAT JUSTICE?

AFTER BREAKFAST I headed for the steam laundry with my dirty clothes, and when the telegraph office opened I was waiting at the door. Ma and Till would hear from me in a couple days. Telegrams were delivered to the Hermosa store.

My report was as follows: ARRIVED IN GOOD HEALTH TELLURIDE SAT PM STOP REASON TO BELIEVE H&P HERE STOP TALK TO MARSHAL SOON STOP STAYING AT OMA OLESON'S BOARDING STOP OWEN

I was on my way out when I ran into the girl from the bakery. She was accompanied by her mother, strikingly beautiful and tall, with the same jet-black hair as her daughter. Evidently the girl had shared everything I told her at the bakery. Her mother was intensely curious about my mission in Telluride, and she was warm and welcoming.

We had a flurry of conversation, her mother and I, the girl following closely. Without a doubt the woman was taking the measure of me, trying to see into my soul, it felt like. I liked her; she reminded me of my mother. I just kept to who I was, like I'd always been taught. At the last, though, I was suddenly off balance. On the spur of the moment, her mother invited me to go to church with them. I stuttered and sputtered and finally agreed to meet them at the Congregational church.

Turning away I was mighty unhappy with myself. I'd been raised to be polite and respectful but also to stand on my own two feet. I could have politely and firmly declined.

At least I'd learned the girl's name—Molly Dobson. Her mother's name was Marie.

I had an hour to spend. Half of it I put to good use eyeing the mules, none of them ours, in the last of the morning's pack trains upward bound to the mines. Then I went meandering around the streets of Telluride, nearly abandoned on a Sunday morning. More than a few drunks were sleeping it off in alleys strewn with liquor bottles. I located the marshal's office but remembered the warning I got at the stables. I decided I better wait until I had a case to make. After church I was going to meet up with Merlin Custard at the town cemetery for the noontime funeral of Elias Eriksson. Merlin was going to show me Uncle Jacob's grave. That would be my chance to learn about his death. Then I would rent a horse and head for the Tomboy Mine in search of Hercules.

As I approached the church at the appointed time, I spotted Molly with her parents and she gave me a quick wave. Her mother's smile was warm, but I could see right away I was making nothing like a good impression on her father. I wondered if he was always this red in the face. Maybe his starched collar was too tight on his neck, skinny as it was. "Decker Dobson, editor of the *Daily Journal*," he announced stiffly as we shook hands. "I'm not surprised that the tracks of your stolen mules led to Telluride. This town has no end of thieves and swindlers and worse. We've got thirty-one saloons and gambling houses, not to mention other dens of iniquity, and only two churches. Does that tell you anything?"

I didn't know what to say to that. Molly looked embarrassed. If her father noticed, it didn't seem like he cared. "And you came here on your own?" he continued, not the least bit friendly.

"Yes, sir," I replied. Dozens of the congregation were passing us by on their way into church. I was saved from further explanation when Molly's mother said, "Shall we go in, Decker?"

Molly's father took her by the arm and led the way inside. I followed alongside her mother, who whispered, "Do you have a denomination, Owen?"

"The Friends," I whispered back. "I'm a Quaker."

The right side of the church was near to full with townsfolk dressed in their Sunday best like the Dobsons. On the left side were men without families, dressed more like me. I was overly warm and more than uncomfortable. I went through the motions, standing up and sitting down with the congregation, but I didn't know one hymn from another and didn't sing along. Quakers of our traditional kind don't sing hymns, and we don't have a priest or a minister.

The best way to get through this, I figured, was to put myself in a meeting house state of mind. I reflected on my Inward Light, and then my family. I was remembering what we were like when Till was born, how happy Ma and Pa were, how thrilled I was at having a kid brother, Till taking his first steps, and the first time he rode a pony, all smiles. Somehow that led to the awful memory of Pa taking sick, and before long, all I could think about was our mules and our dismal situation. The crook was keeping Peaches to ride when he already had a horse. Why was that? This much I knew: the Tomboy Mine bought Hercules. I had to find him before they took him underground.

Something brought me out of my reverie. The minister was giving his sermon and was talking about the importance of acceptance, something to do with Colorado's supreme court. A recent ruling, I gathered. From the far back and across the aisle a man cried out, "Is that justice?"

The young minister was startled. So was everybody. The whole church was murmuring. Molly's father, seated between us, was beside himself. I couldn't tell if he was going to blow his top or melt into a puddle. "Socialist," he seethed in a stage whisper. "Anarchist!"

The minister said in the direction of the voice from the back, "You're welcome here, friend, but you're not welcome to speak out of turn."

One more hymn and the service was over. The church emptied out to a glorious autumn day, but nobody seemed to notice. The well-dressed folk stood buzzing in clusters as the working men drifted away. "His mistake was to bring up politics," I heard a woman say.

I stood aside, waiting to see if Molly might explain what this was about. Suddenly her father came at me very red in the face. To shoo me away from his daughter, was all I could think. "What are you waiting for, boy? Go back to Durango!"

I replied to his conniption fit with a shrug and a smile and "It's a free country."

Rather than return to his wife and daughter, who'd seen and heard the above and looked mortified, the newspaperman hurried to join a heated conversation at the hitching post.

Molly said a quick something to her mother, then walked over and said, "I'm sorry my father wasn't civil, Owen. That's just the way he is, always angry about something. See the man he's talking to over there? That's Arthur Collins, the company's superintendent at the Smuggler-Union. The other is the president of the bank. My father despises the miners even more than they do."

Starting back to her mother, Molly said over her shoulder, "I'll look for you tomorrow . . ."

"That's right," I said. "I owe you a nickel."

I had some time on my hands before the funeral and broke one of my silver dollars at a soda fountain on Colorado Avenue. Lone Tree Cemetery is east of town before you reach Pandora, the man told me. I spent a nickel on a soda and another on the *Daily Journal*.

I found a bench outside and looked into this newspaper run by Molly's father, curious if I might find something about the decision from the state's high court. I didn't, but spotted something about a miner toward the end of Decker Dobson's gossip column: *Just when we think we've had enough of anarchists and socialists we learn of a miner in Oklahoma who refused to march in a parade. Some of the crowd fell on him, beat him severely, and were about to lynch him. We applaud their patriotism. There is no better deterrent to anarchy than mob justice. To fix the problem of anarchists in America, all the anarchists should be deported to some cannibal island. We feel pity for the resident cannibals, eating such disgusting food.*

I felt sorry for Molly. I tossed her father's newspaper in the trash, where it belonged.

11

SO MANY GRAVES

HALF AN HOUR later the funeral procession was headed my way. It was led by a two-horse wagon with the remains of Elias Eriksson in a simple pine coffin. The man sitting next to the driver was Merlin Custard. The men walking behind who'd worked in the mines looked like they'd been through a war. One was missing a hand, several an arm, one of them an eye. Many were hobbling, many were coughing, all were silent and grim. At a nod from Merlin I fell in with them.

Colorado Avenue became the wagon road I had followed into town. Somehow I hadn't noticed the cemetery on the slope above the road and below the cliffs. I was recruited to be one of the pallbearers. The pine box was lighter than I expected. Eriksson must have been a long time wasting away with miners' consumption.

Graveside, it was Merlin who presided. His frail voice was nearly drowned out by the echoing thunder of the stamp mills up the road. "Elias was born to a large farming family in Sweden," he began. "Like many of us, he left his native land to seek a better life in America. Many of you worked with Elias, as I did, and knew him to give every ounce of his prodigious strength until it gave out. Let it be remembered that his friends were many, that he had dreams, that he was a proud member of our union. And now his life is at an end, and we gather to say good-bye and farewell, and wish him eternal rest."

Merlin opened his Bible. "The Lord is my shepherd," he began, and they all joined in. Every man knew the twenty-third psalm by heart. Evidently they recited it frequently. I was so deeply moved, my voice barely escaped my lips.

Afterward Merlin took me up a winding path through the hillside cemetery. It cost him a considerable amount of wheezing and puffing but he was determined to show me where Uncle Jacob was buried. "So many graves," I said when he stopped to rest.

Merlin nodded. "Aye, for a town with such a brief history. And plenty more are unmarked."

As we wended our way, I read some of the nearby stones. TAKEN BY THE ELEPHANT proclaimed the letters under an Italian name, a man who lived only twenty-six years. Under a Celtic cross, the dates on a family stone told a heartbreaking story. The young mother died the day after her newborn child.

I began to wonder if Uncle Jacob had a headstone. *Don't act disappointed if he doesn't*, I told myself. *Ma will take care of it. We can wire money to Merlin once I get home.*

Merlin brought me back to the present. "Here he be."

Jacob's mound had settled and grass had mostly claimed the dirt. I was looking at his name in granite:

JACOB HOLLOWELL
Stalwart of Local 63
Kansas-born   Died 2-17-1900

The brutal reality of it hit me full force. The loss of my father's adventurous younger brother was no longer an idea in my head. The sudden horror of his death hit me full force.

Merlin was teary-eyed. "It's a small stone, but does it please 'ee?"

"Truly," I replied, all broken up. "Ma will be happy about this."

"Our local paid for it," Merlin added proudly. "Few of us could afford one."

We sat down either side of the headstone. The view was magnificent, from the fresh-born San Miguel River

74

to the jagged peaks above. Down the valley lay Telluride, and in the far distance, the La Sal Mountains in Utah. "Same as me," Merlin said, "Jacob came to Colorado on his own hook, as a prospector. Both of us ended up working for wages. A man has to eat." Suddenly Merlin had a coughing fit. It left him gasping for breath and blue in the face.

"I'm sorry," I said when the fit subsided.

"Don't be."

"Your mine must help out . . ."

"How so?"

"With doctor bills and such."

Merlin looked at me fiercely. "Not to the tune of a penny. What makes you think that?"

"The name, Smuggler-Union. Isn't it owned by the union?"

He laughed bitterly. "A mine owned by the miners, that'll be the day! It's owned by a syndicate of tycoons back East. Robber barons! When you get sick or busted up, the mining companies could care less. Without help from our union, most of us at Oma Oleson's wouldn't have a roof over our heads."

"So, where did the mine's name come from?"

"Two claims, the Smuggler and the Union, combined into one. The Union was named by the prospector who made that discovery. I heard it said he fought for the Union in your Civil War. As to your uncle's union, that's our Western Federation of Miners. He was a member in

Cripple Creek when they successfully bargained for the eight-hour day. They were the first to win it."

"Uncle Jacob wrote about that, the same letter when he told us he was heading farther west, to Hermosa. We got a letter once a year around Christmas. In the next one we learned he'd built a house on the land and was working in a mine near Silverton. We never heard why he quit that job and went to work over here in Telluride."

"Well, he didn't quit. He got fired for talking miners into joining the union."

"He never wrote about that."

"I'm not surprised. He knew your father was bad sick, and likely didn't want to upset him. When Jacob came over the mountain to Telluride, he tried to find work at the Tomboy, where management won't raise wages but agreed to the eight-hour day. No luck—jobs there are hard to come by. That's how he ended up with us at the Smuggler-Union, where we work ten hours a day and often twelve until we remove a quota of rock—six feet high, six feet deep, and as wide as the vein. 'Fathom mining,' it's called, and the veins here are unusually wide."

Merlin coughed up some crud and hawked it contemptuously. "I worked under that system back in Cornwall. What I can't fathom is why such a travesty of justice would be allowed in America. We thought we'd finally won the battle last year, when the state assembly passed the eight-hour workday in the mines, smelters, and blast furnaces, and the governor signed it. Then

Colorado's Supreme Court pounced on it, killed it by unanimous decision. Declared the new law unconstitutional. Ruled that working men have the right to work as many hours as they please, for as little pay as they like!"

Merlin had run out of breath. I said, "So that's what the minister was talking about this morning."

"Minister?"

"At church."

He looked at me curiously. "I thought you folks were Quaker."

"We are, but I met a girl . . ."

The old miner had a good laugh. "That explains everything! I must say, Owen, you're a fast operator."

I felt the blood rush to my face and was about to explain.

"More credit to you!"

"I'm trying to understand . . . Did Jacob die before or after the court made that ruling?"

"After. He found it dumbfounding. We all did. Victory was ripped from under our feet. After that the mine superintendent said there'd be no more talking with our union, not about the eight-hour day and not about our wages, working conditions, safety, any of it. Arthur Collins is his name. From England, to my shame. Won't give an inch. Says his responsibility is to the officers and owners of the corporation, not to us."

"So, what's to be done?"

"That's what we were asking ourselves. Our

leaders—young Vincent St. John and your uncle Jacob—
were saying we needed to consider going out on strike,
and preparing. That's when both of them became targets, I believe."

"Any proof that Uncle Jacob was pushed?"

"Sadly no, but we have our suspicions, beginning
with the company man who searches our lunch pails
for high-grade ore at the end of every shift. Your uncle
was alone on the lift when he came up from below. An
accidental fall defies comprehension. This we believe:
rather than talk with Jacob Hollowell, they silenced him
forever."

12

THE NOTORIOUS SMUGGLER-UNION

ONCE WE PUT our backs to the cemetery and headed for town, Merlin told me I better hurry if I intended to rent a horse and make it to the Tomboy and return before dark. I took off at a run for Rogers Brothers. Around three in the afternoon, mounted on a sorrel mare, I started up the trail to the mines.

Too narrow and rough for wagons, the trail climbed steadily through the band of red rock before it turned sharply into and out of a ravine with falling water. The aspens were gold, their leaves fluttering pretty as you please. The mare had no tricks up her sleeve, nor was she ruffled by the steady stream of riderless horses and mules, mostly mules, squeezing by us single file on their way back to town.

Before long there was nothing but air on our right as the trail started across a cliff ledge, heart stopping for me but business as usual for the mare. I snatched glimpses of the view. Down below lay Pandora with its mills and tramways. Beyond Pandora, on the heights of the closed end of the box canyon, there was the tall waterfall where I'd stood on the brink the day before. Ingram Falls, as I came to learn.

Here came some more unattended mules, reins looped around packsaddle forks, about to crowd us over the edge of the cliff. I held my breath and hung tight until the mules and the danger passed. When I praised my ride, the mare gave me an eye roll as if to ask what I'd been so nervous about. In my defense, the drop may have been a thousand feet. She took me through a tunnel and over timbered crib works that supported the trail across an especially perilous narrow spot. With the crossing of the cliff behind us, the trail climbed steeply through the dark spruce forest. On account of the grade and the thin oxygen, the mare's breathing was labored. I let her take her time.

Above eleven thousand feet the air had a wintry chill to it, and yesterday's snow hadn't melted. At a fork in the trail I glimpsed one of the major mines, apparition-like, high above on the mountainside. The mare stopped for a rest pending further instructions. I watched the big iron buckets in motion to and from the mine's tramway station. Coal was coming up, ore was going down.

Behind me, riders were ascending the trail. I waited to ask the name of the mine up above. It turned out that my apparition, perched on the edge of oblivion and backed by solid rock, was the notorious Smuggler-Union where my uncle died. The riders were returning from time off in town. They were miners who worked the night shift. Their rented horses would return to the stables on their own.

The most you could make was three dollars a day, Merlin had told me, with a dollar deducted for room and board. "Wage slavery," he called it. These men must have known my uncle and lived and worked alongside him. Pa's brother had written us about his three-story boarding house. Two hundred men lived in it year-round, through the long and brutal winter. They had electricity, steam heat, a lounging room with a big open fireplace, a post office, a bowling lane and pool tables, a library, and packrats. The food was decent and the coffee was "fit for removing boiler scale." I was about to tell them who I was but held back. It was enough that Merlin and the rest of the men at Oma's knew.

"Looking for work?" asked one of the miners.

I thought he must be joking but wasn't sure. "Looking for my mule that got stolen and sold to the Tomboy," I answered.

"Good luck to you," another said. "Mules too long

underground go blind."

They pointed the way and I took my leave. The trail to the Tomboy crossed the creek, angled up to a ridge, and turned the corner into the next basin. Before long I came to a sign high atop a metal pole wedged among the rocks. BEWARE THE BIG ELEPHANT, it said. I recalled the tombstone I'd seen hours before. Local humor, I decided.

Suddenly the Tomboy came into view, the settlement and the mine works, clustered on a flattish patch of mountainside under the peaks. Echoes of industrial thunder surprised my ears. Sure enough, the Tomboy Mine had its own stamp mill and reduction works, as well as a tramway. As Merlin would explain that evening, having their own mill meant they no longer sent raw ore down the tramway to Pandora, only concentrates. The mine was owned and capitalized by Europeans of immense wealth, the Rothschild family. According to rumor, the Tomboy had recently added its own retort and would soon be making gold bullion in small amounts. As for the Big Elephant, that was the Tomboy's nemesis, a monstrous snowslide that ran across the trail several times a winter, taking lives nearly every year.

I wondered if the Tomboy's blanket of new snow meant winter was here to stay. The place was so high up, it gave me a nosebleed just looking at it. Stunted spruce here and there were the only greenery to be seen.

Within sight of the shaft house where men and mules

were lowered into the earth, I tied up in front of the stable. I was thrilled at the prospect of finding Hercules but daunted by the battle on my hands. I intended to have my way.

The barn doors stood wide open. Comforted by the familiar smell of hay and animals, I wandered inside. To my left, the door to the office was open. A man had his back to me and was talking on a telephone, which surprised me no end way up there. As yet, I'd never spoken on one. "Did I hear you right?" I heard him say. "Seven hundred pounds? You got to be kidding."

I went deeper into the barn. It had eight stalls on each side. Above, on three sides, the loft was chock-full of fresh-baled hay. There were four horses in the stalls, no mules. The mules were all underground, I figured.

The Tomboy's stableman appeared from his office, eyes down and deep in thought. He was bowlegged, from years in the saddle I supposed. His mustache hadn't been mowed in months. From one moment to the next, he noticed me standing there. "Can I help you?" he said, surprised and somewhat annoyed.

"I hope so," I replied, nice and friendly. The stableman heard me out, granite-faced except for a flicker in his eyes when I said that the Tomboy had bought my family's stolen mule. I proceeded with an exact description.

"Weighs fifteen hundred pounds?" he scoffed.

"Yes, sir, his mama topped a ton, and his daddy was

the biggest donkey there is, a Catalonian mammoth. Both from Missouri, where they breed the best mules."

"Sonny, I ain't laid eyes on the animal."

"Do you suppose they'd let me go down in the mine and look for him?"

He laughed. "Not a chance in blazes. No unauthorized personnel—far too dangerous. Take my advice, kid, cut your losses and catch the next train to Durango."

This was the second time in a day I'd been told to go home. I thanked him, for what I didn't know, and asked his name. "Tatters," he said grudgingly, "Fred Tatters." As I swung into the saddle I was thinking of appealing to the mine superintendent, but thought better of it. More than likely, I gathered, Hercules was still in Telluride.

I rode down the mountain into the glare of the setting sun without noticing a thing. I was in a blue funk at the whole situation and angered over the injustice of it all, especially the likelihood that Jacob was murdered. It was dusk when I returned the mare to a surly hand at Rogers Brothers. When I asked when the packers would be rigging mules in the morning, he begrudged me two words. "First light," he said.

Too late for supper at the boarding house, I found something to eat at a backstreet restaurant, the cheapest thing on the menu. Slumgullion stew, they called it. Till would've called it slop. I was up at first light, having slept in fits in Oma Oleson's front room before giving up and reading a couple chapters of the dinosaur book

84

Pa had given me. Oma found me trying to sneak out the front door and insisted I eat "a quick something." In a minute's time she was cracking eggs, and I left on a full stomach.

I posted myself at the head of Oak Street, and over the next couple hours I kept my eyes on the pack trains heading up the trail to the mines. The mules were carrying everything from bagged flour and canned goods to lumber and hay and boxes of dynamite. Hercules wasn't among them. And where was Peaches?

At least I had something to look forward to that Monday morning—paying off a debt.

13

THE GENTLE GIANT

THE LINE AT the bakery was out the door. Molly, with her hair tied back and wearing an apron, was working the counter. Her mother appeared now and then from the back to replenish the breads and treats behind the glass. Glued to the conversation of two men right behind me, I lost track of time. "Darndest thing I ever saw," said one of them. "They lowered it onto his back with a chain hoist. Seven hundred pounds on the back of a mule! Three hundred is standard, and the most you ever hear of is four hundred."

Seven hundred pounds. Now I knew what Tatters was talking about over the phone.

"What's the load?" asked the second man.

"A single piece of cast iron, part of the new compressor for the Tomboy. They broke it down into parts, but this one couldn't be broke down any further. They're going to put the compressor back together up at the mine's machine shop. You should see the mule, brought in for the occasion, I heard. He better be as strong as he is big—the John Henry of mules!"

"This I gotta see. How's the animal taking it?"

"Kicking and breathing fire!"

This didn't sound like our gentle giant, but it's not in a mule's nature to suffer fools. I was going to have to see for myself.

"Think it can be done?" I heard over my shoulder.

"That much weight, a six-mile climb in air that short on oxygen? No, sir, I do not. It's lunacy."

The line had dissolved in front of me. "Owen," Molly called, and I stepped to the counter. Distracted as I'd been, I hadn't even looked at the pastries. I was at a loss. "What'll it be?" she asked with a bright smile.

"Have any apple strudel?" I managed.

"Apple strudel it is!"

Molly made change and I gave her back a nickel. "You remembered," she said. "Wish we weren't so busy . . ."

"I'll be back. I may have just heard something about Hercules."

"Good luck, then!"

Outside, I waited for those two men and followed

them past some warehouses and up Oak Street. A crowd was gathered in front of the New Sheridan. I heard the squeal of a frightened, angry mule. I had little doubt it was Hercules.

And it was. His ears were laid back, his tail was up, and the whites of his eyes were showing. His feet were dug in and he was going nowhere. The man on horseback attempting to lead him was cursing and yanking on the halter rope. Two men with switches, one on either side, were drawing blood on his rump. Pa would have rolled over in his grave.

While hiding Hercules, they'd built a contraption meant to enable him to carry seven hundred pounds up the mountain. The bell-shaped hunk of iron, the core of the Tomboy's new compressor, was nested in a special-made packsaddle. Its most curious feature was an oversized carpenter's sawhorse with a wide top centered under the load. The legs on either side were a few inches short of touching the ground. No one there that day, I imagine, had seen the like. The whole rig looked nothing short of ludicrous.

My first instinct was to shout to high heaven and run to Hercules, but mules don't take to yelling and shouting. Instead I stepped from the crowd and said, "Stop that!" to the men goading him from behind.

At the sound of my voice, Hercules lifted his jackrabbit ears and swiveled them around. His head followed suit.

"Her-cu-les!" I called, and he answered, his long whinny ending with a plaintive hee-haw. His ears tracked me as I came alongside, and when I stood before him, they pointed straight at me. I reached out my hand to his muzzle. He blew out a snort, took in my scent, and nickered. "Hercules," I said, "I'm so glad to see you, and so sorry."

I dabbed at my tears, patted his muzzle, and scratched behind his ears the way he liked. I knew him from the black fringes inside those ears to the white rings around his eyes, to every eyelash. Oh, how I loved him. He rubbed his great Roman nose up and down my ribs, making sounds new to me, doleful and questioning. *Where have you been?* he was asking. *Look what they've done to me!*

The packer leading Hercules wheeled his horse around. "What do you think you're doing, kid?"

"He's mine," I said. "I'm taking him home."

"You're doing nothing of the sort," he snarled.

The crowd murmured their disapproval. Some were looking to a man who stood apart, watching with an expression I took for sardonic amusement. He was imposing, tall and brawny, rugged and broad-shouldered. An older man but not an old man. There was a star on his vest and a gun on his hip. So, this was Jim Clark. The vest and the Stetson hat were dark brown, his trousers a lighter brown. Like his badge, his bushy mustache was dull silver. He looked like a character out of one of Till's dime novels.

Hercules relaxed, bending at the knees, and when he did, the four legs of the sawhorse met the street. For the time being, the weight was on the sawhorse instead of his back. He crouched, resting, waiting for what came next. I thought the marshal would intervene but he was staying out of it. True to his reputation, "a difficult man."

The packer raised his voice. "I have a job to do, kid. They need this load up at the Tomboy and they need it today. I can see the animal has taken a shine to you. Maybe you can help. Either do that or get out of the way."

"It's too much for him to carry. And besides, he's never packed a day in his life. He's a plow mule."

"Are you going to help, or what? We think he can do it."

There's no stopping them, I thought, but I could prevent them from mistreating him. Hercules might even succeed if I went along. I said, "I'll help if I get to talk to the mine superintendent when we get there."

"All right, then."

"You promise me it's a deal?"

"Ain't that what I just said?"

I told him to call off his dogs—the men with the switches—and I took the halter rope in hand. I had a little talk with Hercules. I told him I believed in him and spoke more low and soothing words of encouragement, but I had my doubts. Mules are creatures of habit, and

Hercules was used to pulling a plow with me behind him, reins in hand, doing the driving.

I coiled the halter rope, positioned myself a bit ahead of him and to the side, and called, "Let's go! Let's go!" like we always do when it's time to pull.

No sooner said than done. Hercules rose on his legs, took all that weight on his back, and followed me up the street to the cheers of the crowd.

The packer, having nothing better to do, rode ahead with glances over his shoulder. I suppose he thought he was showing me the way. I didn't care what he was thinking as long as he kept his end of the bargain. If we made it all the way up to the mine, that is.

The crowd and the men with the switches followed us as far as the head of Oak Street, where the trail took off. From there on Hercules wasn't so nervous, and that was a good thing in light of the cliffs ahead. It doesn't take much to startle a mule. As Pa would say, their deepest instinct is self-preservation, widely mistaken for stubbornness. A bit of burlap flapping on a barbed wire fence might be a harbinger of doom. Water of unknown depth might be hiding a crocodile.

As the trail steepened, Hercules was breathing hard and fast, but that was to be expected. He knew when he needed to stop and settle and get that awful weight off his back. The first time he rested, I checked his flank for Pa's omega. Our brand had been smeared with mud that had dried and flaked, and I could see through it to the work of the running iron. The bottom of the omega had been closed to make it into a tall hat, and a bar had been added above.

When Hercules took the weight again, I encouraged him with "Let's go! Let's go!" and we were on our way. Never once did I pull on the halter rope. Every now and again he would stop and point those big ears toward some perceived danger. A little reassurance and we were on our way. Hercules was doing it for my sake.

The tunnel and the cliffs didn't faze him, nothing did. As long as I was by his side, he was good with it. I sang his favorite song for him three times through, "I've Been Working on the Railroad." We didn't have to deal with oncoming mules and horses. Someone had telephoned ahead and told the mines to hold them back until we came through with the extra-wide rig.

Approaching timberline and the fork to the Smuggler-Union, I was having my doubts. Hercules was new to the mountains yet here he was up in the thin air, climbing steep grades above eleven thousand feet with seven hundred pounds on his back. He was streaming sweat and breathing so fast, so loud and heavy, I was afraid his great heart would burst.

At the creek, Hercules took a long drink. We still had a mile or two to reach the Tomboy, and there could be no unburdening him until we got there. *This is my fault,* I thought. I made the wrong call. They wouldn't have gotten him out of town without me.

"Let's get a move on," the packer snarled.

"Why don't you suck eggs," I snarled back.

Once we angled over the ridge, the climbing wasn't as steep. Hercules gave me a grunt and a groan and a sigh. The Tomboy came into view, its early blanket of snow having all but melted since the day before. I called louder now, in the jubilant tone Pa would use to encourage the team when the task was daunting but the end was in sight. The big fellow responded with a surge of Herculean strength. Somehow he had more to give, knowing the end of his ordeal was at hand.

A small crowd was waiting for us—men, women, and children. I heard high praise for Hercules. Indeed, they were astounded and cheering. At the machine shop they had a chain hoist ready and made short work of lifting that infernal hunk of iron off his back.

The bowlegged stableman was there, Fred Tatters, who'd pretended only yesterday to know nothing. "Good job," Tatters said, patting me on the back. "Let's head for the stable. He needs water and a rub-down, and some good feed."

"I was promised a talk with the superintendent," I said.

"First things first," replied Tatters. He was right about that. I followed him to the stable. On the way I stopped and showed him the fresh burns added to our omega brand. They were plain as day. The mud was gone, washed away by sweat. Tatters shrugged and said straight-faced, "I'm not seeing what you're seeing."

"Any fool can see it!" I cried.

He smirked and said, "So, what does that make you?"

Trying to keep a grip on myself, I went in search of the mine office while Tatters led Hercules to the barn. At the office, the assistant said, "Who said you could talk with the super?"

"The packer. We made a deal."

"What packer?"

I'd barely begun to explain when the pencil pusher cut me off. "Whoever it was, he didn't have the authority. The super has bigger fish to fry. Anything having to do with horses and mules, you'll have to talk to Fred Tatters over at the barn."

I told him I'd been double-crossed, and left mad as a hornet. Outside, I looked around for the packer. Already left for town? Where was the crowd that hailed us, anybody who might help? They had evaporated, every single one.

I hurried back to the stable, intent on collecting Hercules and putting the Tomboy behind us. Hercules was deep in the barn with his muzzle in a grain bag. The hulking man grooming him looked like he knew his way around mules. I approved of him using a brush rather than a metal currycomb, but all the same I resented him fiercely. "Not too much grain," I said. He glared at me, didn't say a word.

94

Tatters was in his office. "I'm taking Hercules," I announced.

"I wouldn't advise it," he said, a grin showing under his droopy mustache.

"Why is that?"

"Big Herm's got his orders."

"Who's he?"

"My stablehand. He's good with animals but not with people. Don't try to reason with him—I guarantee you he'll lose his temper. Break your arm or worse."

"Okay, I'll reason with you."

"Be my guest."

"You lied to me, Mr. Tatters. Yesterday you said you never laid eyes on the animal."

"At the time that was a true fact."

"Well, you'd just heard about him over the phone. You lied."

"I did no such thing. Seeing is one thing, hearing's another. Now, the Tomboy's got a bill of sale—"

"From a rustler! It's phony!" I was on the verge of calling him a crook for playing along.

"Look, kid, I've got a job to do. If you got a beef, take it to the marshal."

"I will, and soon. Just tell me you're not going to hide Hercules underground."

"He's too big for tunnel work. We bought him for packing jobs like the one today. Until they make the trail into a wagon road, we're going to need him. Let's not make a habit of these little talks, eh?"

"There's no chance you could've got that piece of machinery up here without me and you know it."

"Nobody's going to remember what you did today, kid, they're going to remember the mule. Welcome to mining country. Now beat it."

14

FIRE ON THE MOUNTAIN

FROM BREAKFAST AT the boarding house Tuesday morning, I went directly to the marshal's office and was invited by a deputy to warm a chair. I was remembering the marshal's poor behavior on the street the day before. It was clear to the crowd and high heaven that the mule was mine, yet he wouldn't lift a finger. Somehow I had to convince him to take Hercules from the Tomboy, find out where Peaches was, and go after the rustler. More than likely I'd seen the culprit going into the bar Saturday afternoon. He might still be in town.

I'd only been waiting a couple minutes. The clock on the wall said 7:45 when a man in grimy overalls burst through the front door, wild-eyed and gasping. "Fire at the Smuggler-Union! It's bad, real bad!"

His shouting rousted the lawman from the back. Marshal Clark was wearing his Stetson and gun belt. Jim Clark listened intently as the miner told his story. The fire might've started at the stable. It spread quickly to the tramway platform and the covered works at the mouth of the Bullion Tunnel. Everything was going up fast with huge volumes of oily black smoke. There was talk of blowing up a building to keep the fire from reaching the boarding house. During this whole account I was thinking of Hercules. Thank God he wasn't at the Smuggler-Union. He was out of harm's way at the Tomboy.

"Any loss of life?" was Clark's first question.

"Not that I know of."

The marshal's gun belt had my attention. His hand cannon was an ivory-handled Colt .45. "Injuries?" he inquired.

"Don't know. It was all happening fast, and there was so much smoke. The phone line to town went down. Hardly any water for fighting the fire."

"So, plenty of property damage. We know that much."

"The Tomboy is sending a crew over to help."

Just then the marshal noticed me sitting there and cast a withering glance at his deputy. Needless to say I got shooed out in a hurry. I'm pretty sure he recognized me from the day before, on the street with Hercules, but he could've cared less. With this emergency on his hands, I had a bad feeling I wasn't going to be able to plead my case anytime soon.

On the street everything felt ominously calm, but within minutes people were out on the boardwalk pointing high to the north. The cloud of smoke was awful black. I wondered if Merlin Custard knew, and what he might have to say. On my way to the boarding house, there were a lot more people craning their necks. They'd heard that the fire was up at the Smuggler-Union.

I found Merlin in the backyard with some of his Cousin Jacks, as the Cornish miners were called. Looking skyward toward the inky, billowing smoke, they were engaged in highly agitated conversation with overtones of dread and undertones of anger. As fast as they were speaking, their brand of English was a whole other language. I waited on a bench nearby for Merlin to come and explain.

When the men went indoors for coffee, Merlin sat down with me. "Heard about the fire, have you?"

"When I was waiting to see the marshal."

He wiped his forehead with a handkerchief. "This could be bad, Owen, extremely bad. If that smoke got in there—"

"In where?"

"Into the tunnel, down the shaft and into the drifts."

"How could the smoke get into the tunnel?"

"From natural suction. Mines breathe, same as caves. The Bullion Tunnel can be downright windy. That's what the men were talking about just now. Given the smoke and confusion, I'm afraid we haven't heard the whole story."

"Were men working inside?"

"The night shift—around a hundred."

"I met some of the night shift Sunday on their way back to work."

"Now you can pray for them. Back in '78, twenty-seven men lost their lives in a bad snowslide above the Bullion Tunnel. This could be worse."

From top to bottom, as Merlin explained, the Smuggler-Union was nearly two thousand feet deep. The Bullion Tunnel accessed the main shaft about halfway down. These days it was the main entrance for the miners, and it was where the ore came out in carts to be sent down the tramway. Where the tunnel met the main shaft, the men rode the hoist cage down to the lower levels—a thousand feet down to the ninth level at the bottom. "That's where the men were working when this happened," Merlin said.

"You think it's likely the smoke got in and went to the bottom?"

"I fear the worst. A lot of what's probably burning— the boiler and all its fuel, the engine, the converter—sit as close as fifty or sixty feet from the tunnel. Disasters have happened at other mines where the portal is wide open, with no doors to keep fire and smoke from getting in. Our local has been pleading for iron safety doors that could be quickly lowered in an emergency. Arthur Collins won't even discuss it. He's so cheap, and if our union is for it, he's against it."

My Cornish friend went silent a few minutes. No doubt he knew the men who might be trapped. When he spoke again it was to say, "From the ninth level, they might be able to climb the ladders to the seventh. From there, if the smoke isn't too bad and they can breathe, they might be able to escape out the Sheridan Tunnel. Time will tell, Owen, time will tell."

Soon thereafter we were among hundreds standing in the middle of Colorado Avenue in front of the New Sheridan Hotel. The mountain was still smoking and everybody was waiting for news. When the news came, it was devastating. So great had been the oily smoke and the confusion, thirty minutes went by before the foreman of the newly arrived Tomboy crew, suspecting the worst, discovered the dense smoke rolling into the tunnel. As more than likely it had been doing since the fire started.

With this revelation, Telluride's world turned upside down. For a few minutes everyone was too stunned to speak. Then most of them ran every which way, to tell someone or to try to do something. The worst had come to pass, and the town was horror-struck. That included me, though I was only a visitor. I was still worried for Hercules, but reminded myself that the terrain up there was above timberline, with nothing but rock between the two mines. There was no way the fire could spread to the Tomboy.

Minutes later, men on horseback were clattering up Oak Street. Merlin pointed out the town doctors, the editor of the *San Miguel Examiner*, and young Vincent St. John, the president of the Miners Union. They were followed by thirty or more men on foot, most of them in miners' overalls. Some wore helmets with carbide lanterns.

We heard more news from the Smuggler-Union. The fire erupted not in the stable but on the tramway platform, where a few men roomed in a corner of the rig. Their heat stove was the culprit. They were in their bare feet and ran for their lives. The conflagration raced through the dry buildings, claiming everything but the store and the boarding house. When the tramway station crashed, the cables lashed the ground with tremendous force in a long swath that included a section of the trail. By a stroke of luck no one was in the path of destruction at that fearful moment.

There was so much yet to be known. How many victims? How many survivors?

When Merlin headed back to Oma Oleson's, I wandered the streets aimlessly, lost in morbid imaginings. Immersed in the general gloom, I was sitting on the banks of the San Miguel when, out of the blue, a girl in jeans took a seat on the grass by my side. "Molly!" I said. "How did you—"

"I saw you heading this way."

"You've heard?"

She nodded mournfully. "Time is going slower today than I can ever remember."

With the stream burbling a pebble toss below, we spoke of the unfolding disaster. Molly knew more than I did. At her father's newspaper office, some good news had finally come in. There were survivors from the smoke in the mine, maybe as many as fifty. In the smoke and by the light of their carbide lanterns—the electric lights were out—they managed to climb two hundred feet up the ladders from the ninth level to the seventh, where they escaped out the Sheridan Tunnel just like Merlin had hoped. Others never made it that far. The smoke was so dense and so suffocating, some of the men climbing the ladders could no longer hold on. They fell to their deaths after crying out in warning to the men below.

We were both overcome with the imagining of it. After a sorrowful silence Molly asked after Hercules and Peaches and what brought me to Colorado. I spoke of leaving Kansas and ended with the events of the day before. She'd heard talk in the bakery of a mule that carried seven hundred pounds up to the Tomboy. "So, that was Hercules!" she marveled. "What a magnificent creature!"

I learned that Molly and her mother had their own horses—her mother's sorrel and Molly's blue roan. A few days before, Molly had taken them to the farrier for new shoes. "Are your mules shod?" she asked.

"Their hooves are so hard they don't need them."

"Up here they do, the ground is so stony. Yesterday, when you were with Hercules, did you notice?"

I didn't, I admitted.

"Here's what I'm getting at. I'm guessing Hercules and Peaches have both been to the farrier, probably ours. He does a whole lot of business. Maybe you can find out if Peaches and the rustler are still in town."

I was already rising to my feet. "Good thinking!"

Just then we heard the huffing and chuffing of a train pulling out of the station. We ran up the bank and across the tracks in advance of two locomotives paired to pull the afternoon's passengers and freight over Lizard Head Pass to Durango. We darted up a side street to avoid the black smoke and the shower of cinders.

15

THAT OLD YARN

"BACK SO SOON, Miss Dobson? One of them new shoes causing your roan trouble?" Molly's farrier, iron rasp in hand, was working on a chestnut mare.

"Nothing like that," Molly said. "I brought a friend who's looking for his mules."

As I described Hercules and Peaches, the farrier kept working. I felt like I was on a short clock and didn't mention their brands. Henry Tompkins had the torso and arms of a heavyweight boxer. He'd recently shoed a great big brown mule for the Tomboy, he said, and a gray with a spotted rump for a man he'd never met.

"What did he look like?"

"Had a black beard and a slouch hat, said next to nothing and paid in advance. A lean fellow, chewed tobacco, carried a gun. I took him for a cowboy in town for a spree. Some of 'em prefer a mule's gait. The motion is easier on your backside."

"But that wouldn't explain the gun."

"Some of them beef drivers don't feel properly dressed without one. But I didn't catch your point."

"He pulled that gun on me. He rustled those mules."

Tompkins set his rasp aside, heard me out, and shook his head in disgust. "That's a dirty business. He prob'ly blew town the day before yesterday, soon as he collected your gray mule. Have you talked to the marshal? There's nothing he loves better than tracking down rustlers, and I don't believe he's had the opportunity in some time. Hates riding a desk."

"I tried to, right when the disaster broke. He's tied up with all that's going on."

Molly had something on her mind. "About the marshal," she said to Tompkins, somewhat tentative. "Were you here in June of '89?"

"I was, but what are you getting at, Miss Dobson?"

"That he was out of town the day of the bank robbery."

"You mean, that he was in on it with Butch Cassidy, and collected a bribe that Butch left under a log? The marshal was overdue for a day off. Surely you don't believe that old yarn."

"My father doesn't. He says people want to believe it because of rumors from places the marshal had been before. Father says all the best sheriffs and marshals have a violent past."

"That's a known fact. Jim Clark keeps this town safe, even if his methods aren't always by the book. Telluride is rough enough as it is. It would go back to wild and woolly without him. He's mighty good at crackin' noggins."

I thanked him for his time. The farrier said, "Good luck finding your animals!"

Out on the street, I thought of something that might be keeping the thief in town. "Molly," I said, "does Telluride have a saddlery, one that makes saddles from scratch?"

"Only Angelo's. What are you thinking?"

"If the thief intends to ride Peaches like he said, he must know that he needs a special-built saddle. He wouldn't get far without one—a mule is built different."

Molly was chuckling. "What's funny?" I asked.

"How I'd love to see him get bucked off!"

The saddle shop was only minutes away. "We go to Angelo for horse tack and repairs," Molly said.

"If he's making a saddle for Peaches, I hope he's taking his time."

"There's a lot of work in a saddle, and he's a perfectionist. Angelo made a new bridle for me recently. Father mutters every time, says we shouldn't patronize his business."

"Charges too much?"

"Because he's Italian, and Father hates Italians."

I was plumb speechless. "Oh," I said.

"Mother told him the horses are our business—hers and mine."

"Why Italians?" I ventured.

"For no good reason!" Molly was about to say more, but we were at Angelo's door.

The saddle maker was a smallish man with spectacles. Angelo looked more like a watchmaker. He was at work on a mule saddle. "A wonderful animal," he said when I described Peaches.

I was beside myself. Molly and I exchanged glances. Peaches was still in town. I was getting somewhere!

"She was curious when I was measuring her," Angelo said, "but she didn't give me a bit of trouble."

"That's Peaches," I said. "We named her for her sweet disposition." When I told Angelo that Peaches was stolen, he said he expected as much. The brand included fresh burns and the man was a brute.

The artisan kept working, barely looking up as he spoke. "I told him it takes me three weeks to make a saddle and I have other customers. *One week*, he demanded. I haven't slept in two days! He came back this morning and gave me another double eagle extra. Sixty dollars for a saddle! It better be ready Sunday, he said. With engravings and rifle scabbard, no less. He had a gun—threatened my life! Don't tell anybody,

Molly. Only if something happens."

When Molly said he should talk to the marshal right away, Angelo said he wasn't going to make trouble: "It's a lot of money for my family." I was about to explain how much my family stood to lose but held off. Soon as I got the chance, I'd try to get the marshal to come talk to Angelo. There was still time—five days. Clark wouldn't have a reason not to, and Tompkins had said the marshal liked to get after rustlers.

Outside, Molly said she needed to spell her mother at the bakery. Tomorrow, though, was one of the days her mother had help. "Do you have plans?" Molly asked.

"I need to talk with the marshal, but there's no chance of that tomorrow with all that's going on."

"We could take a ride up to Blue Lake. The horses need the exercise, and I'd really like to show it to you. What do you think?"

"I'd love to, but will your parents—"

"Mother will be all for it. After church, they had a spat over what Father said to you. She reminded him it was she who invited you to church, and then she quoted the verse from the New Testament: 'I was a stranger . . .'"

Molly paused, wondering if I might finish it.

"'. . . and you did not take me in,'" I added.

"That's the one! Mother said she believed you were a person of upright character."

"I'm glad to hear it. What if your father needs the other horse?"

"He's scared of horses."

"Still, he wouldn't like the idea."

"True, but he doesn't have much say."

All of this was somewhat astonishing, but so was Molly. I'd never met anyone like her.

16

BLUE LAKE

IN THE MORNING Molly was out in front of the boarding house at 8:00 a.m. sharp. I adjusted the stirrups on her mother's sorrel and we were off. As we rode side by side through the streets of Telluride and east toward Pandora, I asked if she'd learned anything new about the disaster. "All but twenty-four men are accounted for," Molly said. "There's very little smoke left, so the recovery begins this morning. They're hoping some of them might still be alive somehow, but it seems unlikely. Mother said it was a good time for us to take this ride and get away for the time being."

I wondered if her father knew, but I didn't ask.

As we clopped abreast of the cemetery, I was pondering the dead silence from Pandora's thunderous stamp mills. Molly saw me thinking and said, "The mills are all closed today to honor the dead. The mines, too— the Tomboy and the Sheridan, the Nellie and the Liberty Bell, and the Flora-Japan. Even the mines over at Ophir and Alta. None of the men are working today. Come to think of it, the same goes for the mules."

I appreciated her thinking of Hercules.

From the head of the valley, we followed a trail that climbed toward the brink of Bridal Veil Falls. "Three hundred and sixty-five feet!" Molly declared. "Tallest waterfall in the state!" Closer yet, we rode through a rainbow in the mist.

From the top of the falls, we had a fine view across to the tramways and the electric transmission lines climbing steeply from Pandora up to the mines. The tramways were shut down, all their buckets standing still. The snowy peaks encircling Telluride, almost close enough to touch, looked dazzling in the crystalline air. "Enjoy it while the mills are closed," Molly said. "No smoke, no haze—what a day!"

The trail followed Bridal Veil Creek higher and higher, in and out of the trees. My guide on her blue roan led the way. We climbed higher yet, above the tree line and onto the tundra. The trail swung up and around a waterfall. After that climb I was in suspense, thinking I would spy the lake any second. Molly rested the horses on the false summits, not saying a word, just beaming. The breeze was cool but the autumn sun had some warmth to it.

When Blue Lake appeared at last in its stony bowl, its hue was a brilliant aquamarine. Still as glass, its surface mirrored the vaulting peaks that surrounded the depths in a horseshoe. I was mesmerized.

A smile was playing on Molly's lips. "Not an eyesore, eh, Owen?"

"More like the eye of heaven!"

"It's a beauty, and the closest to home. The San Juans have more than a hundred high lakes, every one a jewel. I've made it to seven so far, the other six on foot. One so high I had to climb hand over hand."

"Sign me up," I said.

Her mother had packed a picnic lunch complete with a tablecloth, which we anchored with stones on a patch of grass where the creek spilled from the lake. French bread and cheese, a sausage and a pear for each of us, and apple juice. Molly asked after my father and I told her we lost him to TB. She wanted to know if he was kind. "In every way," I said.

"That's how it should be," she murmured wistfully. Abruptly, her tone changed. "Owen, I'm sorry for Father's rude behavior. Mother won't abide that sort of talk at home, and now he's calling people names in church. His editorials and gossip columns are, well—"

"I read some of it. Mob justice and lynching—was he serious?"

"It's awful—don't read it! Read the *Examiner*. They're sympathetic to the miners, while he calls them anarchists, socialists, and revolutionaries. He especially despises their union."

"But why?"

"Mother believes it comes from his own insecurity. She says it's the way of the world. The poor and the wretched are despised for their poverty and wretchedness. She cringes when he toadies up to the rich and powerful, in print or in person. I've heard her try to reason with him. Of course the miners need to speak with one voice."

"That's what my uncle always said."

"How else will they ever improve their lot? They're under the lion's paw! Now look what's happened at the Smuggler-Union, as if they don't have it bad enough."

"Has your father always been like this?"

"Mother suspects as much. They rushed into marriage—never, ever do that, she tells me. We came here seven years ago from Chicago, on the strength of her inheritance. Her parents were both gone; her father had owned a very successful factory."

"You mean to say, your father married for money?"

"Love and money, I suppose. They bought the bakery and the newspaper with her money. I was too young to notice but Mother says it didn't take long before he was writing with a poison pen. He's been getting worse and worse. It's like a disease!"

It was shocking to hear a daughter speak this way of her father, but I had met him. We spoke of many things after that. I was about to turn sixteen and Molly already had. Both of us were facing trouble and had so much on our minds. She said I looked like a duck out of water in church and wondered about that. Molly had heard from her mother that I was a Quaker, and was curious about me knowing the Bible but not going to church. I explained that we have the meeting house instead. Anyone might bring up a religious question. Usually there's a lot of discussion, sometimes very little. On occasion the meeting is silent and thoughtful from beginning to end, with each of us looking to our Inward Light for understanding and answers. Molly was intrigued, and wondered if there were a lot of Quakers in Kansas.

"In eastern Kansas, quite a few," I said. "The good soil brought them, but there was more to it than that. My mother's grandparents migrated from Pennsylvania to Kansas Territory to help the Shawnee people become farmers, and Pa's came from Iowa to add voters who favored the territory becoming a free state. There were other people coming to Kansas who wanted it to be a slave state."

"All I knew was, the Quakers wanted to abolish slavery and were opposed to all wars."

"Except one," I said. "When it came to the Civil War, they were of two minds, since the Union soldiers were fighting to put an end to slavery. Some Quakers fought.

Ma's father gave his life in the 'Gettysburg of the West,' the Battle of Westport in '64. Pa's father was a pacifist and stayed home. Even so, the war came to him. He was gunned down in his cornfield by one of Quantrill's Raiders."

We went on to compare favorite books—*Wuthering Heights* and *Huckleberry Finn*—and I got to talking about *Behold the Dinosaur*. How a teacher and minister in Morrison, Colorado, by the name of Arthur Lakes had discovered *Stegosaurus*, *Apatosaurus*, and *Diplodocus*.

"Not to mention *Allosaurus*!" Molly exclaimed. "The gigantic predator with teeth like steak knives!"

"You know about Arthur Lakes?"

"He was here last month! There was so much interest, they had to move his appearance from the library to the Miners Hall."

These days, Molly explained, Lakes was a professor at Colorado's School of Mines and the editor of *Mines and Minerals*. "You should've been here!"

"I would've asked him why there aren't any fossils in these mountains. I've been looking."

"Somebody did ask. The San Juans are young and volcanic, he said, and burst through the older sedimentary layers from the time of the dinosaurs. For a good long while, these mountains were unspeakably violent. Where Silverton sits in that huge bowl, an enormous volcano blew itself to bits!"

The wind had come up, the horses were restless,

and the day was getting on. "The lake's going to freeze over before long," Molly mused. "I guess it's time we go, before it does."

Our hours together had gone all too quickly. As we rode down Bridal Veil Creek, it felt like my time in Telluride was running out. I was already missing Molly. I doubted I would ever meet the match of her, so spirited and intelligent.

Molly's mother had been right about us needing to get away for a spell. Reaching Bridal Veil Falls, we caught sight of a dreadful scene across the way. Teams of men were carrying the dead, wrapped in sheets and roped to stretchers, down a tremendously steep trail to Pandora. As we drew close they were loading the bodies onto freight wagons. At the sight, our high-flying youthful spirits came crashing down. The coroner was having them sent to an empty warehouse in Telluride.

17

NOT MUCH FOR PAPERWORK

THURSDAY MORNING FOUND me filling out a report at the marshal's office. "No, you can't speak with the marshal," a lout of a deputy told me. He was a different lout from the one who shooed me out Tuesday.

I went to work on the document but was having my doubts about the town coppers. In hopes of catching the marshal coming or going, I kept one eye on the door with his name on it. I intended to jump up and have my say. To my surprise, here he came—through the front door—and I seized my chance. I rose to my feet so fast, his right hand went to his holster and he nearly drew his weapon. "What's the matter with you?" he snarled, his voice raspy as sandpaper.

I came to the point and said it forthright. "My plow mules got stolen."

I'd startled him, and Jim Clark was still angry. "You're a pine-blank idiot, kid. You nearly plowed your last furrow."

"I'm sorry, Marshal. I was hoping to get your attention."

With his boot heels striking the wood floor, he came at me and clamped his heavy hand between my neck and shoulder. I looked up and met the marshal's steely brown eyes. His face was as hard as a block of quarried limestone. For an older man he had amazing strength. His grip tightened like a vise, about to break my collarbone. "You got my attention," said the lawman, and let go. *Same here,* I thought.

Clark doffed his Stetson. The marshal's full head of brown hair was graying at the temples, and his silver mustache was stiff as a push broom. He hadn't shaved in some time; his whiskers showed more salt than pepper. "What's that?" he said, indicating the papers I had in hand.

"The report I just wrote."

The marshal took the papers with my drawings and all, and with a jerk of his head led me to his office. Inside, he closed the door, hung his hat on the rack, and dropped my report in the trash. "I'm not much for paperwork," he drawled, possibly with a hint at humor. I sat where he pointed, the chair facing his large oak desk. When the brawny man took a seat in his desk chair and leaned back, its springs complained for lack of oil. "Keep it brief and entertaining," he said.

I thought, *Till could handle the entertainment better than me.* I said, "When you saw me on the street the other day—"

The skeptical rise of Clark's eyebrows stopped me short. I couldn't believe he was pretending he didn't remember me.

"I'm the one who got the big mule moving, right out here on Colorado Avenue. He's mine. His name is—"

"Back up," the marshal scowled. "Start with *your* name."

"Owen Hollowell."

"Where you from?"

"Hermosa."

"Outside of Durango."

"Correct."

"Born there?"

"Born in Kansas."

"Kan-sas," he drawled. "Western, middle, or eastern?"

What's this about? I thought. Hadn't he said "Make it brief"?

"Eastern," I replied. Trying to help things along, I told how we brought our mules with us in July, only to have them stolen in the wee hours of Tuesday, the twenty-fifth of September.

"Go on," Clark said, mildly interested, keeping an eye on the door. I was getting maybe a third of the marshal's attention. A couple of times he glanced at a large photo on his desk among some other clutter. The photo was of some men dressed up fancy. Something about them seemed to amuse him. I had no idea what was funny. From where I sat they were upside down.

When I got to the part about the thief pulling his gun on me, the marshal said, "Now, that's entertaining, Owen Hollowell. Judging from all that scribblin' in yonder wastebasket I reckon you're a writer. Is your tale fiction?"

"No, sir, it's the unvarnished truth."

The marshal stroked his chin stubble. "In the dead of night?"

"The moon was full."

"And you didn't have a weapon."

"That's correct."

He broke into a skeptical smile. "You've got sand, I'll give you that much."

"I was desperate. We're plumb ruined if I don't get them back."

Finally he heard me out. I fished my drawings out of his wastebasket and showed the marshal our omega brand and how it had been changed into a bar over a hat. I told him I'd explained the same thing to Fred Tatters and showed him the fresh burns, that Tatters could see full well that the Tomboy had bought a stolen mule.

"More than likely," I added, "Tatters already knew their bill of sale was phony."

To all of that, the marshal didn't say a thing. He studied my drawings with his mouth turned down at the corners, which didn't bode well. Then he got out a book of Colorado livestock brands, spent a couple minutes turning pages, and closed it. "There ain't a brand in here with your omega or a bar over a hat. The Tomboy's got possession, and there's a lot to possession being nine-tenths of the law. You'll have to wait until the 1901 book comes out in December. We'll find out if the Bar Hat is a new and legal outfit. No way to say the Tomboy's title to the mule isn't good until then."

I tried to object, going on about both mules, but he wasn't having it. "As for the gray mule—your notion that I have a deputy stake out the saddle shop—I haven't got a complaint from Angelo. I suggest you keep your eye out for this alleged rustler you think you saw going into the Sheridan. If he's mounted on your mule, let me know. The district attorney pursues cases that will stick. Short of that I suggest you go home and let me take care of things proper. I don't cotton to rustling."

Still, I wasn't going to give up. "He might have Peaches hidden out of town somewhere. Do you suppose I might talk with the county sheriff, and see if he might—"

"Go right ahead," said the marshal. "He's up Disappointment Creek out of Slick Rock, looking into a murder."

"Where's that?"

"The far west end of the county."

"How far is that?"

"Eighty-ninety miles."

Out on the street, I felt like I was twisted into a knot. There must have been a way I could've said it better and got Clark on my side. Till might've won him over. All I could do now was try to catch the thief with Peaches. *Sunday at the latest,* I thought. *The louse will have her in hand when he comes to Angelo's for the saddle. He'll saddle her on the spot to make sure everything fits just right.*

I went to the soda fountain and tried to settle down with a strawberry soda. They had the daily and weekly newspapers side by side, and I knew which one deserved my nickel. SMUGGLER DISASTER was the headline on the special edition of the *San Miguel Examiner.* There was much in the account that was new to me. From the top of the shaft high on the mountain, two men volunteered to ride the cage down to the seventh level in hopes of rescuing the men from the ninth. The two were supposed to ring when they got there but the ring never came. When the cage was brought up, one man was dead and the other wasn't long for this world.

Billy Hutchinson, the foreman of the crew from the Tomboy that raced over to help, was the one who discovered the fatal smoke flowing into the Bullion Tunnel. As quickly as possible, he oversaw the explosion to seal the portal.

Vincent St. John, the young president of the Miners

Union, was credited with numerous acts of heroism. After braving the smoke and the flames to attach a hose to a water line, St. John climbed over a ridge and entered the mine by an abandoned entrance in hopes of saving men trapped inside. He made it two hundred feet through the smoke before being turned back. Once recovery efforts began, he worked tirelessly to bring out the bodies of the dead and stretcher them down to Pandora.

In the EVENTS AND ANNOUNCEMENTS section, I saw that the miners were honoring the fallen at 8:00 p.m. that evening in their union hall. The day following—Friday—there would be a community procession to Lone Tree Cemetery followed by the funerals. The procession was to begin at 9:00 a.m. in front of the courthouse.

I picked up the *Daily Journal*, curious to see if Molly's father made any mention of St. John and his heroism. Here, I thought, was a chance for him to redeem himself, especially in the eyes of his daughter. There wasn't a single mention.

18

CRIES OF PRIDE AND GRIEF

WITH EMOTIONS RUNNING so high, Merlin told me, the Miners Hall would be packed that evening. When I said I was hoping to go, Merlin didn't hesitate. "Jacob would want you there. What's one more sardine in the can?"

Merlin wondered if I'd been able to talk with the marshal. "I did," I said. "It wasn't exactly a conversation. It felt like cat and mouse, and he was the cat."

"He's the cat, all right, and he's been jumpy as one lately. Talk has it he's got four Winchester rifles ready at certain locations around town. He's always had enemies, but more so since he got his job back."

"I got the idea he's a fighting man."

125

"Of the first order, fists or guns. He's a crack shot with revolver or rifle—the fence out at the cemetery is his personal shooting range. Certain letters in the signs are his targets. When he first came to town, back in '87, Telluride wasn't like you find it now. I mean to say, it was rough."

"How rough?"

"Well, the rowdies and the bandits were running wild and shooting up the place—had a regular reign of terror going. When Jim Clark came to town, he was digging ditch for a pipeline. In the midst of a ruckus, he walked into the mayor's office and said he would arrest the malefactors if he had a badge. And he did, without firing a shot."

"But how?"

"Cracking the toughs up the side of the head with his six-shooter! He marched them to the clink and that was that. Jim Clark got my vote in the special election for marshal. He became a fearsome presence on horseback or patrolling afoot. At the same time he was making extra money as a bill collector. Down from the mountain, in town socializing or gambling, you'd get a tap on your shoulder. Uh-oh, it was the marshal. All he'd say was the name of the merchant you owed money to, which meant you better pay up quick. Clark is nothing if not an enigma. On occasion he helps the needy and the old folks. Does chores, makes repairs."

"Yet he shows no interest in helping me," I said bitterly.

"Nobody knows what to expect from Jim Clark. Likes to keep you guessing."

"So, what do you make of the talk about him being in on the bank robbery in '89?"

"In cahoots with Butch? A lot of folks believe he was, me included. That's not the only story in that vein. He may have done some moonlighting in various disguises as a hold-up man. Typically the victims were on their way out of town after withdrawing their money from the bank. He was also rumored to be on the take when stagecoaches with gold shipments were robbed. Such-like suspicions, along with his foul temper and brutal treatment of prisoners, led to his firing after the Butch Cassidy robbery. His history before Telluride is murky, but he's said to be from Missouri and to have fought with Quantrill's Raiders."

"Who burned Lawrence, Kansas, in '63," I shot back. "That's where I'm from."

"War is madness! The marshal makes no bones of having fought for the Confederacy. He's proud of it."

"Where did he go when he was fired?"

"He turned up in Leadville later in '89—got shot in the leg, we heard, in some kind of altercation. It came to light he had two felonies on his record dating back to his teens. Seems he stole his stepfather's mule and lit out with a friend for Texas, where they traded the animal for six-shooters and stuck up a rancher for fourteen hundred dollars. You Americans are nothing if not colorful.

By '93 the ruffian crowd had taken over Telluride again, and the powers that be gave him his badge back."

Needless to say, this conversation gave me plenty to chew on regarding the man who might or might not help me recover our mules. If Clark would take it on, he was the right man for the job. As to Hercules, I could pretty well guess the marshal was beholden to those "powers that be" that Merlin alluded to, including the Tomboy Mine. Come December he would have to do something when Colorado's new book of registered brands was published. In the case of Peaches, it sounded like he might be willing to do something sooner. I could picture the marshal busting our skunk up the side of the head with his revolver. Such were my ruminations as I made my way to the telegraph office.

Here's what I came up with, to the tune of a half dollar: SPENT MONDAY WITH HERCULES STOP GOT A LINE ON PEACHES STOP TALKED WITH MARSHAL STOP WISH ME LUCK STOP

My message was less than forthcoming but what could they expect from a telegram? It would've cost a chunk of my funds to tell Ma and Till what was really going on with Hercules. Everything was so complicated and uncertain, and I didn't want to worry them. I felt bad about leaving the mine disaster out of it, too, but they could read about that in the *Durango Herald*.

That evening, the atmosphere in the Miners Hall was dense and electric. Dense, in that it was crowded with twice as many men as comfort would have allowed. The board of Local 63 called the meeting to honor the dead, but every man there was expecting more, and that expectation is what I mean by "electric." The sorrow every miner was suffering was coupled with anger. *Rage* would be more accurate, over the absence of metal doors that could have sealed the mouth of the Bullion Tunnel when the fire broke out. Was the board going to call for a strike?

To my astonishment they brought me up on the stage to stand with the board. With great solemnity they read the roll of the dead, citing each man's birthplace and what was known of his family. Most came from across the ocean, most were unmarried. There were cries of pride and grief from their countrymen as their countries were called.

I'll never forget what it was like to be looking at that sea of faces. From that day forward, laboring men who work the dirtiest, most hazardous, and most thankless jobs would never be faceless to me.

After the roll was called, one of the board members stood up to make an announcement. "Some of you may be wondering," he said while pointing me out, "what this kid is doing here." The throng buzzed over that a bit, and then he said, "This here's Owen Hollowell from Durango, nephew of *Jacob Hollowell.*"

At that I got the same reception I received at the boarding house, multiplied a hundredfold. Fortunately all I had to do was wave.

Then the president of the union was announced to a thunderous ovation. It went on for a good long while. They were hailing Vincent St. John for his courage.

When the cheers subsided, the hall got quiet as a churchyard. "I'm going to be brief," their young leader began.

"Don't forget those doors!" a voice called.

"We'll have them for certain," St. John replied. "Arthur Collins is away on business in Mexico, as some of you have heard, but the acting superintendent—his brother Edgar—says we have his word."

A ripple of contempt ran through the hall along with strong approval of a victory won, if at appalling cost.

"This isn't a time for rancor," St. John said forcefully. "Nor is it time for talking about a strike, though that may come, as all of us know. This is the time to honor our friends. This is the occasion and now is the time, your elected leaders believe, to do something fitting in memory of them. Something that will stand the test of time."

The man's person, his bearing, his voice . . . there was something you couldn't put your finger on, but Vincent St. John had the ability to reach into hearts. "All the losses we've suffered," he continued, "as you gray-beards know all too well . . . the cave-ins, explosions gone wrong, electrocution, snowslides and rock slides, miners' consumption, pneumonia, the deadly roll call goes on and on. Is there an occupation more inimical to

130

health and downright dangerous than ours? No, there is not. Dr. Hall's hospital has done wonders for its size, but the population of Telluride and its environs, counting the men up at the mines, is pushing five thousand. In light of this new calamity of fire and smoke, we have to ask, what if dozens had been injured? It's a shame that Telluride is so unprepared and so lacking. A crying shame!"

I heard cries of agreement and anger, but mostly the members were wondering what St. John was getting at.

"Here's what we're thinking, men, and we're hoping you'll agree. The town won't levy taxes for a new hospital, and the mine owners won't even contribute, much less foot the bill. Who does that leave but us? Out of this tragedy, with your consent, is born a vision. Paying for it over a period of time will mean sacrifice from every one of you, but this will be our legacy: a forty-bed hospital with room for seventy in emergencies. We can afford it if we build it with our own hands . . . *the Miners Union Hospital*!"

For a few moments there was dead silence. Then, like a swelling wave, their approval rose to a mighty roar.

St. John went on to ask them, as they left the building, to sign a declaration of intent. They waited patiently to reach the tables and sign. The result was overwhelming.

The funeral procession the next morning reached from the New Sheridan Hotel all the way out to the cemetery. A band led the way, followed by the labor organizations from Telluride and Ophir. Then came Telluride's citizens in carriages and afoot. Newspapers across the country would report more than four thousand people in attendance, including the miners from Ouray who came by train.

The services were solemn and mournful. A hymn was followed by scripture, a prayer, and homilies by Telluride's minister and priest. A second hymn was sung as the caskets were lowered. Vincent St. John read "The Miner's Farewell," and the minister gave the benediction. The band played a stately dirge as the throng was ebbing away.

I was among the stream of humanity making the mile-long walk back to town. Up ahead, a shaggy-haired kid was walking in spurts against the flow, slowing to scan the faces. As he drew closer I couldn't believe my eyes. It was Till.

19

THE FORT WORTH FIVE

"TILL!" I EXCLAIMED, surprised and then some. *"What are you doing?"*

"Lookin' for you," he panted, hands on hips.

"But how'd you get here?"

"By train. I left my stuff with Oma Oleson. She told me you was at the funeral."

"But why'd you come?"

"Came to help you find H and P, what else?"

"Well, thanks," I said with little conviction. "Hercules is way up on the mountain. He got sold to one of the mines. I haven't seen Peaches."

"I just did."

"You lie like a rug."

"Really, Owen. I really did, when the train was pullin' in."

"You sure?"

"Sure I'm sure."

"What'd you see?"

"The varmint you descripted, beard and hat and everything. He was ridin' a dark horse and leadin' Peaches. I'm dead positive it was her."

"Did she have a saddle on her?"

"Yep, but no rider."

"That saddle wasn't supposed to be ready until the day after tomorrow!"

He looked quizzical. "I'll explain later," I said. People were bumping into us from behind and we stepped aside. "Which way was he heading?"

"The opposite of the train. Leavin' town at the outskirts."

"We should go to the saddle shop. The crook might've said something, like where he was headed."

We fell back in with the mourners returning to town. I was annoyed with how much I was going to have to explain.

Close on my elbow, Till asked, "Why don't we go tell the marshal how I seen Peaches?"

"We will, and soon, but first you've got some explaining to do. Does Ma know you're here?"

"She put me on the train. Sent me with fifteen dollars."

"What for?"

"Ten for a headstone for Uncle Jacob if he ain't got one, five in case you're short."

"Come on now, I can't picture her sending you by yourself, not knowing for sure I was even still here."

"Well, I convinced her."

"How?"

"Said I'd walk if I had to, like you did, but I was going one way or t'other and there weren't no way she could stop me."

"Till, you rascal, you can't do that."

He bit on his lip. "I reckon I did."

"So, why didn't Ma come with you?"

"She's got a job."

"Ma's never had a job."

"Does now. She's the hotel manager at Trimble Hot Springs. Even got a cottage so she don't have to go back and forth on Queenie."

"So who's taking care of Queenie?"

"They got a stable at Trimble."

"I'm gone hardly more than a week, and all this?"

"You know Ma. She said she had to grab the bull. We're between the devil and the deep blue yonder, right?"

"I'm afraid so. Let's send her a telegram so she knows

135

you got here and found me. Then we'll talk to Angelo at the saddle shop. See if we can learn anything about the rustler before we see if we can talk to the marshal."

The telegram sent, we went straight to the saddle shop but found it closed. Angelo's daughter was there cleaning up. He'd gone home less than an hour before, Francesca told us, plumb exhausted. He'd been working day and night making a saddle for a customer with a bad temper.

I said, "I thought the saddle was due Sunday."

She shrugged. "Papa wanted to get it over with and the man kept paying extra."

Till thought he'd put in his two cents. "We need to talk to your pa."

"Maybe he's not asleep yet. Let's go see."

They lived close by. "Papa was so sorry to miss the funerals," Francesca said on the way. "I just got back. So sad."

Angelo was sound asleep. Little brother was in my ear, saying we should get Francesca and her mother to wake him up. I said we should find the marshal. That was music to Till's ears.

I expected we'd have trouble getting to the marshal if he was even there. I'd seen him at the funeral. Chances were, he was meeting with dignitaries or something.

Turns out he was in his office. I asked the desk clerk if we could have a word, and the clerk went to see him. I was expecting a firm no but had to keep trying.

Marshal Clark appeared at his door. He looked us

over, his steely gaze on Till instead of me. Till's eyes were on the marshal's gun. "Come in, boys," the marshal said with a grin.

The marshal pulled an extra chair in front of his desk. I introduced my brother and said he just got in from Durango. "Till," Clark repeated.

The kid spoke right up. "Short for Tillson, Marshal."

"Owen and Tillson, the Hollowell boys."

"Call me Till."

"How old are ya, Tillson?"

"Ten come January."

"Nine, is that it?"

"Yes, sir."

I'd barely begun to bring the marshal up to date when Till, never one for sitting still, popped out of his seat. He went to looking around the office at the framed pictures and wanted posters and such. When Till came back, he stood at the marshal's shoulder and squinted at the photo on his desk, the one with five men dressed up fancy in a photography studio.

I thought for sure Clark would swat him away. He was thinking about it.

Till pointed at the one seated on the right. "That's Moneybags!"

At this, I came around the desk for a look. "That's him," I agreed.

"Who's Moneybags?" queried the marshal.

"Tell him, Owen!"

To the marshal's amusement, I told him we'd met the man in Pueblo's train yards on our way west, how he wanted to buy our mules, how he was flashing hundred-dollar bills, how we turned him down. We soon learned the source of his wealth, and why the marshal was amused. "Boys, that's the Fort Worth Five you're looking at! This photo just came in the mail a couple days ago. This is the first picture of the Wild Bunch, and they had it taken themselves! Thought they were invincible, I suppose. Look at the smirk on the one you pointed out, like he's got the world by the tail. Eleven years robbing banks and trains and never been caught. The man you're calling 'Moneybags' is wanted dead or alive. That's Butch Cassidy."

Till was all agog. "Golly, Marshal! How you know that's Butch?"

"From his mug shot when he went into the Wyoming pen in '94, for buying a horse he knew was stolen."

"Just think, Owen, Butch Cassidy tried to buy our mules! Look—exact same hat, exact same clothes!"

"At first he was after Peaches," I explained, "for a riding mule."

The marshal's grin was a mile wide. "A mule would be far superior to a horse in that rugged country where he hides out, somewhere over in Utah."

"Robbers Roost," Till said. "Do you know where it's at, Marshal?"

"Wish I did."

Just then I recognized another face in the photo. "Hey, this one's the skunk that rustled our mules. He's got a beard since this picture, but that's him."

Till's eyes went big. "Holy moley. He's the one I just seen with Peaches when I got off the train."

I reminded the marshal, "You said for me to tell you when I saw him with Peaches."

"So I did. This gets more and more interesting. Your thief is Harvey Logan, alias Kid Curry."

"Get a posse!" cried Till.

"Too much sound and fury."

"But you'll go after him?" I said.

The marshal was thinking on it. "I reckon I will."

Till was beside himself. "We'll be your posse!"

"Hmm," Clark said with a sort of a smile. "There might be something to that."

20

ON THE TRAIL OF KID CURRY

THE ONLY TEST the marshal put us through was saddling our horses. "I was born on horseback," Till bragged. To which the marshal said, "How did that work?"

If Clark was impressed with Till's technique of mounting up like a jack-in-the-box, he didn't let on. The horses underneath us were from the marshal's stable, where we met him at first light, like he'd insisted. The streetlights were still on. My mount was a buckskin, Till's a dappled brown colt, and Clark rode a big black. I had taken a shine to a pinto, but the marshal said those white patches would make a good target if I was feeling suicidal.

When Till asked after what the packhorse was carrying, Jim Clark said he was too old to go without his coffee and bacon.

Second-guessing was second nature to Till. "Won't that packhorse slow us down? How are we going to catch up with Kid Curry?"

"Gradually and without raising a cloud of dust," came the marshal's answer. "He doesn't know he's being followed. You boys rise and shine when I say, and we'll overhaul him just fine. Give me guff of any kind and I'll stake you out on an anthill. Understood?"

I believe I heard Till gulp. "Understood," we both replied.

"Keep up the patrols," the marshal told the two deputies who showed up at the last minute to see him off. "I don't expect much crime after a disaster like we just had." Asked how long he might be gone, the marshal replied irritably, "As long as it takes. If the mayor asks, tell him I'm after a mule thief."

With that, minutes after sun-up on the first Saturday in October, we rode out of Telluride: Marshal Jim Clark trailing a packhorse, then Till, then me. The marshal made it clear we would be riding in that order always and without exception.

Why was he taking us along? I could identify Logan, but on the face of it, this was ridiculous. Maybe it was just an excuse to get out of town. Did he have reason to believe somebody in Telluride was about to sneak up on him and blow his brains out? The man was so mysterious and sly, so contrary and unforthcoming, it was impossible to tell. Maybe it was to collect the bounty on Logan. No matter his motives, I had a strong feeling that going along was the only way we stood to recover Peaches.

The early sun was yet to burn off the frost. Like Till, I had the wide collar of my wool mackinaw flipped up against the chill. Just ahead of me, Till tugged at his new hat, which resembled the marshal's Stetson. I tugged on my slouch hat that went back to Kansas. We'd shopped for the things Clark said we needed, including rain slickers, a bedroll for Till, some rope, a fistful of candles and wax-dipped matches, and two canteens, one for Till and the other for a spare. Till found himself a new pocketknife, long-handled underwear, and riding boots. We both bought bandannas to tie around our necks.

Our saddlebags were full to bursting with stuff of our own and items the marshal shoved at us including hardtack, tinned fish, and extra ammunition for his revolver and the Winchester scabbarded under his leg. The leather strings at the backs of our saddles secured our bedrolls and rain slickers, along with our tarp and ground cover.

A couple miles out of town, with the light coming up fast, we came to a fork in the wagon road next to a slaughterhouse and a stockyard with a hundred or more steers awaiting their demise. After ordering us to stay put, the marshal dismounted and walked in both directions, stooping here and there to examine tracks. He chose the road to Lizard Head Pass. Mounting up, the marshal surprised me by asking if I could handle a gun.

"Not hardly," I said, "I'm a Quaker."

"Imagine that," he remarked.

Till said he was a crack shot with his .22 but Ma wouldn't let him bring it.

"A wise woman," quipped the marshal.

The wagon road up the south fork of the San Miguel was a climb from the start. On the mountainside above the hydroelectric powerhouse, nearing a dramatic loop in the railroad tracks, we got smoked by a train from Telluride hauling sacked concentrates to the smelter in Durango. Till was dying to tell me he'd been through here the day before but was trying to show the marshal he could keep his trap shut. I was happy to have little brother ahead of me, where I could keep an eye on him.

On the far side of the pass, we made a stop in sight of the monumental tower of rock called Lizard Head. "No way does it resemblify a lizard," Till declared. "It's scaly, I'll give it that."

The horses snatched at the grass while we lunched on hardtack biscuits and sardines. The marshal lay down on his back, exhaling a sigh. He looked at the sky and closed his eyes.

"I'm gonna see a man about a horse," announced Till. When he returned from watering a tree, Clark was sharpening the big knife he wore on his left hip. Till said, "Is it gonna be in the newspapers about us chasing one of the Wild Bunch?"

"Newspapers?" Clark snarled, bolting upright. "Nobody knows about that photograph but me and you two. Did you boys say anything to anybody?"

Till was letting me handle this one.

Of course I'd told Molly, without even thinking about her father. I doubted she passed it along, since it involved me. "Just an old miner in the boarding house," I answered.

"Who's that?"

"Merlin Custard."

"The Cousin Jack? He ain't the sort to flap his gums to the papers. This is my play, and I don't want nobody butting in, be they law or Pinkertons."

"Pinkerton detectives," Till explained for my benefit. "The most famous one is Charles Siringo. He used to be a buddy of Pat Garrett, the sheriff who gunned down Billy the Kid. He's been chasing Butch and the Sundance Kid for years."

Clark sheathed his knife. "Know a lot about Butch and Sundance, do you, Tillson?"

"I know a few things."

"Where from?"

"From one of them 'Blood and Thunder' books. Butch was a Mormon kid from Utah. His real name is Robert Leroy Parker. Growin' up, he was Bob Parker. He had a butcher job once, so that's where 'Butch' came from."

"What about 'Cassidy'?" I asked.

"Mike Cassidy," Till replied without hesitation. "When Bob was about your age, his family was up against it. His pa kept the farm going while his ma ran a rancher's dairy. It weren't close enough to go back and forth every day. She had to go live there, and she took the boys with her. Mike Cassidy was one of the wranglers—he took Bob under his wing. Told him about his rustlin' escapades, showed him how to throw a loop and use a runnin' iron. Bob wanted to be like him. When he became an outlaw and needed an alias so as not to shame the homefolks, he chose Butch Cassidy."

"Interesting," said the marshal.

"So, where did 'Sundance Kid' come from?" I asked.

"That's Harry Longabaugh," Till said. "He did the sun dance with the Sioux."

"You learn something new ever' day," said the marshal, droll as can be. "All this while I was under the impression it had to do with his prison spell in Sundance, Wyoming, for stealing a horse and a gun."

Till didn't let on that he'd been schooled. The marshal said, "Let's get a move on, boys. I think it's clabbering up to rain."

On his feet, Clark took aim with his big hunting knife at a carving on the trunk of a nearby aspen, smooth as skin. MANUEL + ROSA it said, inside of a heart. He clean missed. "Gettin' old," the marshal groaned.

Before the marshal could take a step, Till ran and

retrieved the knife. Just short of giving the pigsticker back, he stepped to the side, whirled, took it by the blade, and threw it end over end at the marshal's target. By chance the knife stuck dead center between the names. Till let out a whoop and looked to the marshal, expecting amazement and congratulations. All he got was a glare.

It started showering as the road met the Dolores River. We didn't break out our slickers, but it rained enough to make the tracking tricky. Even so, the marshal made out where Logan and Peaches left the road at a trail up Coal Creek. The trail led us over a high ridge to Dunton, an old mining camp with hot springs on the west fork of the Dolores. Clark approached the ghost town with extreme caution, scouting on foot from building to building with his .45 drawn. We waited by the stream until he reappeared and told us the coast was clear. Harvey Logan had spent the night here and so would we.

First thing, we hobbled the horses so they could get after the meadow grass. The whole place had a sulphurous rotten-egg smell to it. The marshal had no interest in the hot springs, but we were eager to take a soak. Inside a dank cabin we tried the concrete tank with steaming mineral water spilling in and out of it. The tank had a ledge for sitting in the water, but we didn't last two minutes. Till said, "This is where they boiled the rotten eggs."

Outside, closer to the river, we found a hot springs pool dammed by smooth stones that was more to our liking. We sat out a rain shower there, perfectly comfortable. I said to Till, "I've been thinking. That was no lucky throw with the marshal's knife. You've been practicing. Where'd you get a pigsticker?"

"Found it in the barn our first day," he confessed. "Musta been Uncle Jacob's. I practice at the big tree by the river."

"What for?"

"I was gonna challenge you to a contest and whup ya. I'm tired of your almighty arm every time we skip rocks or throw at targets. You always win."

"I'm fifteen. You should take that into account."

"Don't rub it in."

"Okay, I won't," I said, trying to keep a straight face.

"If Hercules got sold to one of the mines, how do we get him back?"

I explained about the book of brands and December, and my suspicion that the marshal was on the take from the mining companies, including the Tomboy. Till said we should steal Hercules. "*Take* him," I insisted. "Are you forgetting he's ours?"

"That's how come we're gonna steal him."

"Whatever you say. I'm already thinking about it, if that's what it takes. I'll have to wait until summer, when the snow is off the mountains."

The marshal had a campfire going and was in a talkative mood. It appeared he was going to forgive and forget the knife-throwing incident. We learned that Butch

Cassidy and his two accomplices passed through Dunton on the run from the Telluride job. Till asked Clark if he was the leader of the posse that was chasing them. "Sheriff Beattie was," he replied. "He put a large posse together on short notice. I was out of town. When I got back, they'd already left."

"They never caught up," Till said. "Butch had fresh horses stashed along the way."

"Including this very spot," the marshal added. "Which reminds me of a story. That colt you're riding, Tillson, is a ringer for the one Butch rode the day of the robbery. It was a gift from Harry Adsit, the owner of the Spectator Ranch, a huge spread west of Telluride. Butch cowboyed for him while he was scouting the bank. Ten days after the robbery Adsit got a thank-you letter mailed from Moab, Utah. Butch said that the colt carried him a hundred and ten miles in ten hours over rough country."

The marshal cooked supper—bacon and beans and corn bread—out in the open over a fire. He baked the corn bread in a cast-iron Dutch oven he'd brought along. Dessert was peaches from a can. When Till said he must know a lot about Butch, the marshal said, "I have more than a passing interest. Some people say I musta been in on it with him, and that gravels me no end. Now I've got a chance to nab one of his Wild Bunch."

"That'll show 'em," Till said.

"I reckon it will."

"Where's Moab," I asked, "where Butch sent the letter?"

"It's in Utah, on the Grand River, the biggest tributary of the Colorado. Butch and Matt Warner and Tom McCarty crossed on the ferry there. They were chased across the river through the Arches and beyond. They nearly got caught when they rode into a box canyon by mistake. Got cliffed out—it shoulda been all over. The posse was in such a hurry they rode on by."

I asked if that was the original posse from Telluride. "Oh, no," Clark scoffed, "they'd long since gone home. There were posses from all over. Telegrams will do that."

It was just about dark, and the marshal called it a day. He said we should take advantage of the bunkhouse. I didn't like the idea. We'd already walked through there and it was musty as could be, with rodent droppings all over the place. Some of the mattresses had been robbed of corn shucks for nesting material. But when the marshal moved in there with his bedroll, weapons, and saddlebags, I followed suit and Till along with me. How bad could it be?

Our candles were still burning when the rats appeared. We watched them scurry around, brazen as can be. "They're huge suckers," Till whispered.

"Don't give 'em no never-mind," ordered the marshal. "Just a couple of packrats." He doused his candle. "Put out your lights."

We did. My bed was sagging, a real back-breaker. In the dark, the sound of those rats was intolerable. After a bit I said, "I think I'll sleep outside."

"Sleep where you are!" Clark barked, mean as could be.

I lay awake a good while, afraid of what I'd gotten us into.

The dern packrats kept it up. One of them scurried across my bedroll. What was I going to do?

I felt in my shirt pocket for one of my lucifer matches, struck it on the bedrail, and lit my candle.

"What's up?" Till whispered.

"I can't take it in here," I whispered back. We gathered up our stuff. The marshal, if he was still awake, didn't give us any guff.

21

THE FOUR HUNDRED HORSEMEN

WE HAD A fire going when the marshal appeared in the morning, and if he wanted to wring our necks he didn't let on. He made oatmeal and bacon and eggs, and ate with his back against a big spruce. Coffee in hand and .45 at the ready, gazing at the mountain stream racing by, he looked almost peaceful, like he was on a camping trip.

Till broke the silence. "Marshal, ain't you afraid Logan's gonna git away?"

The marshal poured himself some more coffee. "He's got no idea we're on his trail, and he ain't pushing the animals. You looking for bloodshed, Quaker boy?"

Till was only a little taken aback. "Just askin'."

"Well, you and big brother might want to reconsider. Logan is wanted for the murder of a sheriff in Wyoming last year."

That got our attention. The murder, as Clark explained, was in the aftermath of a train robbery near Wilcox, Wyoming. Wearing masks, the Wild Bunch dynamited two safes and rode off with $50,000, some of it paper currency, a lot of it gold. After they split up, three of the robbers were pursued into rough country outside Casper. The sheriff and his posse located their hideout, dismounted, and nearly caught them by surprise. Without masks, all three came out with guns blazing, and Harvey Logan shot the sheriff in the guts. The other two weren't identified. The outlaws escaped and the sheriff died the next day.

"So, what'll it be, fellas? You still want to be in on this mule chase? Suit yourselves, quit me if you like."

Till glanced my way, and I shook my head. The kid gave our answer. "We're gonna stick, marshal. And if you ain't in a hurry this morning, that don't make no never-mind to us."

That last bit had me amused at Till parroting the marshal's lingo from the night before, but I kept a straight face. Till's pride was easily bruised.

Logan's track led us down the west fork to its confluence with the Dolores River. We were on the main-traveled road again, and Peaches's hoofprints were nowhere to be found. The passage of freight wagons, stagecoaches, and riders had erased them. At the depot in Dolores, the marshal asked an old-timer on a bench if he'd seen a rider leading a saddled mule. The answer: "Yessir, this time yesterday."

Outside of town, where the wagon road began its climb out of the narrow river valley, the marshal spied a trail heading downriver and dismounted to inspect it. His report: "Kid Curry went thisaway."

For reasons of its own, the Dolores was making a sharp bend to the north. The trail kept us on the east side of the river. Here and there the trail was overgrown and hard to find, but mostly we made good time at a slow trot and put a great many miles behind us. It was beyond me how the marshal could proceed without the paralyzing fear of ambush. From behind I could see him scanning to his right and across the river to his left as well as straight ahead, but the task seemed nigh impossible.

If Clark's strategy was to stay a day behind and catch up with Logan in a location more advantageous, that was fine by me. I was after our mule, not excitement.

Thoughts of Ma had me feeling blue. I could've stayed up the night before we left and written her a letter explaining a great many things, but I was thinking we wouldn't be gone very long. I would wire her when we had Peaches. Now that it was evident we might be gone a good long while, I was deep in the weeds.

Whenever we crossed a creek, the marshal paused

to let the horses drink. Other than that we pressed on. Late in the day my funk finally lifted. On both sides of the river, a layer of rock was emerging from the earth and shooting skyward. We were entering a canyon of red rock with fossils to be found.

The newborn canyon of the Dolores River soon rose to a few hundred feet. The resulting shadiness lent itself to ponderosa pines in the draws between the cliffs. Monarchs of their kind grew on the canyon bottom, their trunks three and four feet in diameter. Suddenly the trail steered into the river where it was especially shallow.

The marshal had me hold the packhorse while he rode across the river. He dismounted on the other side and continued on foot with his rifle, disappearing in the trees where the trail appeared to leave the canyon up a timbered draw.

Till and I were eyeing the soft beds of pine needles and hoping the marshal would call it a day. When he got back he did just that, after declaring that Logan had left the canyon.

"I expect he's headed for Monticello, across the Utah line," the marshal said over supper, a stew he cooked in his Dutch oven. He'd brought along no end of surprises: potatoes and onions and carrots, even apples, as well as a pantry of canned goods.

Daylight was dimming as I scrubbed the dishes at the river, but enough remained for me to study the sandstone behind our campsite. I didn't find any fossils but was happy to be looking. The farther we got from the volcanic San Juans, the better. Crossing into Utah was all right by me. In my mind's eye I could see all those sedimentary layers exposed like an open book.

In the morning we climbed out of the canyon and emerged onto a plateau with an immense expanse of sage and juniper before us. In the distance a solitary clump of mountains rose from the plain. The Blue Mountains, the marshal called them. Monticello, he said, sat in front of them.

The marshal lost the track late that day as we pulled into town. Clark headed for the Carlisle Ranch nearby, another spot, he said, where Butch Cassidy had fresh horses waiting after the Telluride heist. We camped on the edge of the ranch. He went to see the Carlisles on his own with that recent photo of Logan in hand, the one of the Fort Worth Five.

When the marshal got back from his visit, it was obvious he'd had a few, or more than a few. His face was redder and his tongue looser. The Carlisle brothers were cagey, Clark reported, but somewhat cooperative. Kid Curry had stayed with them the night before, and out and told them he was headed for Robbers Roost to deliver a mule Butch had taken a liking to. "A crazy stupid mission, but just like Butch," Logan told them. Cassidy's favorite horse had been killed from under him and he wanted to try a mule for some reason.

"So that was it!" cried Till.

The marshal said he asked after which of the river crossings Logan was heading for. There was Taylor's Ferry across the Grand River at Moab, the one Butch had used in '89, and there was the ferry at Hite City, a hundred or more miles downstream on the Colorado. The Carlisles said they didn't know which it was, but after Logan had a few drinks, he got to talking about the gold frenzy at Hite, so the Hite ferry would be their best guess.

Sunrise was working its way down from the peaks of the Blue Mountains as we rode out of Monticello. The aspen stands were glowing amber gold with the sun's early fire. We reached Blanding before noon. When we tethered to the hitching post at the general store, the marshal pinned his star to his vest. Inside, he learned that a man leading a saddled mule had been in the store the previous afternoon.

The storekeeper spread a map on the counter. Clark didn't seem to mind me at his elbow. "The road west begins at this very street corner," the man said. "It looks more like a road on this map than it does on the ground. It's more of a track. Nary a soul lives between here and Hite. It's all rough country."

His description proved true but we made good time. My buckskin and Till's colt had stamina and were thriving on the journey. After crossing the creek in Brushy Basin, we climbed up and around the head of Arch Canyon. Shortly after topping out on Bears Ears Pass, we rested the horses and took in the view.

The marshal brought out his map. The late-day sun was lighting up an immense escarpment on our left, a red wall maybe as high as a thousand feet that ran south as far as the eye could see. Comb Ridge was its name. Our route west from Blanding had jogged around its northern end. Below us, clad in dark green junipers, lay Cedar Mesa. The eastern rims of its many canyons shone golden, most prominently the high cliffs of Grand Gulch on its long and serpentine course to the San Juan River.

We camped that night at the stony edge of White Canyon in view of a colossal natural bridge that spanned the creek at a great height. When Till announced that he was going to climb up and run across it, the marshal remarked, "Ain't enough dirt around here to bury a cat."

With the tension between the two of them rising, Till chewed on that for a silent couple of minutes, until the sudden croaking of frogs gave him an out. He jumped up and ran down to the creek on the hunt for one. I took a walk in the dusk, looking for fossils. I didn't find any but collected a strange rock, purple and perfectly spherical, a third smaller than a baseball but heavier. A concretion, as I later came to learn. I put it in the pocket of my mackinaw for a souvenir.

Supper was "pig out of a can" as Clark called it. He said it was looking like we wouldn't catch up with Logan until Hite City. I asked how big of a town it was.

The marshal said he didn't know, but from the way the Carlisles were talking, the gold rush in Glen Canyon was on for real this time. Hite was the headquarters for a number of downstream operations, including a floating dredge built on site that was more than a hundred feet long.

"You figure Logan might stay over in Hite City?" I asked. "Rest up, gamble, visit the saloons before he goes on to the Roost?"

Clark nodded while chewing on some pork gristle. I was picturing things working out nicely. Hite would have a livery, and that's where we would find Peaches. We would take her and head for home.

Till piped up with "I just figured out how come we been lollygaggin'!"

He'd said it to the marshal, and now he couldn't take it back. If looks could kill, Till would've expired on the spot. He tried to recover with "You reckon it'll be easier to take Kid Curry in town. Right, Marshal?"

I gave Till a hard look of my own. Little brother replied with a shrug.

In the quiet that fell, the pops from the fire were unusually loud. This seemed an especially bad time to have poked the bear. I broke out the reading fodder I'd brought along, my dinosaur book and the recent issue of *National Geographic* Ma sent with Till.

Till went to reading the magazine, no doubt wishing he'd brought along something more exciting. I was deeply absorbed in *Behold the Dinosaur* and wishing I could talk about it with Pa. New discoveries were being made all the time. At a place called Bone Cabin Quarry in the Wyoming desert, so many dinosaur fossils were eroding out of the hills, they built a cabin entirely of dinosaur bones.

I was trying not to notice, but all this while the marshal was staring into the flames. Then he got up and went to his stuff. He came back with a bottle of Old Crow and a shot glass. An alarm went off in my head but I didn't say anything. Till didn't appear concerned. I suppose the whiskey certified the marshal as the genuine article.

Clark went back to staring at the flames, and threw down five shots over the next while. I glanced at his grip on the bottle, and for the first time noticed how uncommonly large his hands were. I imagined the damage they had done, and I imagined him throttling Till's neck. Suddenly he came out with "So, you boys are from Kansas."

Till said, "Yessir, that's right."

"Eastern Kansas, your brother told me."

I nodded apprehensively. The marshal poured himself another shot. "How long your people been there?"

"Before the War Between the States," Till answered proudly. "They were Free Taters."

"Free Taters, no foolin'? Never heard about that. How'd that work?"

"Free *Staters*," I explained.

Till gave me a pained look. "I know what I'm talking about, Owen. Just an expression."

"Nothing to do with free spuds?" queried the marshal with a drunken grin.

Till said, "They moved there so when it came time to vote, Kansas would outlaw slavery."

The marshal lifted his glass and threw down the shot. "So, they were abolitionists."

Till looked at me for help. He'd just realized we were in quicksand.

"Like I told you," I said to the marshal, "we're Quakers."

"So you did, so you did. You come to Colorado from a farm in Kansas—where you had them mules."

"That's right."

"Where exactly in eastern Kansas?"

"Outside the town of Lawrence."

"How far?"

"Seven miles."

"Which side of Lawrence—north, south, east, or west."

I was leery of this, but he was pushing. "East," I said. "How come?"

"Because I rode with Quantrill and Bloody Bill Anderson during the war. You heard of the Lawrence raid, Tillson?"

"Yessir," Till said gravely.

"Tell me what happened."

"You tell him, Owen."

160

This wasn't something I could shrug off. "You're saying you were there?"

"I was."

"Well, Quantrill's men burned Lawrence and massacred a hundred and sixty-some men and boys."

"That many? I'm not surprised. Lawrence was a nest of abolitionists, and we were out for blood, four hundred strong. 'The Four Hundred Horsemen of the Apocalypse,' you might say. I was twenty at the time."

I'm a coward, I thought, *if I don't tell him what happened.* I spit it out. "Our pa's father was shot dead at close range, working in his corn field."

The marshal mulled that over, poured himself another shot, hesitated, and threw the whiskey into the fire. The flames flew up. His features were ghastly. "Just so you know, boys, that might've been me."

We were too stunned to speak. I was picturing the marshal as a young man riding with the mob of rebel raiders as they approached Lawrence, him leaving their flank to slaughter a farmer in his field. He as much as said he killed our grandfather. Not for sure but very likely!

An awful silence ensued as the fire burned to coals. All the while, hatred was invading my mind and soul. As the minutes crawled on, one thing became clear: I couldn't let anger and hatred consume me. I fought back hard. Finally I managed to say, "If it was you, I forgive you, marshal." And Till murmured, "We forgive you, marshal."

Clark laughed. "With malice toward none, is that it? Like the Great Emancipator said?"

"Isn't that the way it should be?" I asked him.

"S'pose so," he said with undisguised sarcasm. "If you say so."

We left Clark to his bottle and unfurled our bedrolls on a sandy spot behind a juniper that was rooted in rock. We could see passably well by the starlight reflected off the cream-colored sandstone. The night was moonless and the Milky Way was ablaze from horizon to horizon. I lay awake, much disturbed at how the marshal had swatted away our forgiveness and made it ring hollow. I had to wonder. What was it like when he rode into Lawrence with the four hundred? If he took part in the horrors there, how could he ever forgive himself?

22

ON THE BANKS OF THE COLORADO

THE MARSHAL'S HANGOVER cast a pall over the morning. After what had happened there was no telling what he might be thinking or feeling. Clark looked haggard as can be, his eyes reptilian. He wasn't talking and we weren't asking.

The wagon track flanked White Canyon as it ran northwest from the Blue Mountains. The creamy white color of the canyon made a striking contrast with the redrock formations above. No stopping for lunch, the marshal was pushing hard. The country turned more arid by the mile, and the heat rose as the canyon descended toward the Colorado River.

Hours later, we followed switchbacks down to the shade of the widening canyon bottom. It felt good to get off our horses. They drank from a stagnant pool as we drained our spare canteen. A pair of ravens was having a lot to say. The marshal wanted his extra rifle shells out of my saddlebags. "You boys stay put," he ordered. "I reckon we're close to the ferry but I'm not sure how far. Hite City's on the other side of the river. I'm gonna go ahead and deal with Logan. I expect he's laying over there."

Clark was finally going to make his move. He wanted it to be in town rather than out in the open. "How long should we wait?" I asked him.

"As long as it takes. Might be tomorrow."

Till piped up with "He's wanted dead or alive?"

"That's right, he is."

As we watched the marshal disappear down the canyon, his rifle out and ready, I must've had a doubtful look on my face. "What's wrong?" Till asked.

"It might not be possible to surprise Logan and take him prisoner. There might be a gunfight. I'm wondering if we'll see the marshal alive again."

"Course we will!"

"I hope you're right. We'll have Peaches back and this will all be over. Someday Jim Clark's luck is going to run out."

"If I had my .22, I woulda gone with him."

"You would, you sure?"

"I'm a crack shot—ask the prairie dogs."

"Sure, but it's a different thing to kill a man."

Till thought about that. "Pa said once it's okay if I'm not cut out to be a Quaker."

"Really, he did?"

"I told him I never seen my Inward Light no matter how hard I tried."

"What'd he say to that?"

"Said I would discover it one day when I wasn't even lookin'."

"Sounds like Pa."

Till's eyes went watery. "I miss him bad, Owen."

"I know it, brother. Think if he could've seen all the wonders out here. He would've loved it so much."

The marshal's packhorse needed unburdening but we decided to stay ready. We staved off our hunger with saddlebag jerky. Dusk was starting to settle as Clark came riding back.

Till sang out, "Did you git him?"

The marshal waited until he drew rein. "Logan crossed early this morning and left straightaway. Let's get a move on. They got the ferry waiting on us."

We weren't long reaching the crossing, where an ancient ruin like a tower stood sentry with a long view upstream and down. The Colorado River in October was less than mighty. It was dwarfed even further by the immense world of bare redrock it ran through. As for the city on the other side of the river, I couldn't make one out.

We led our horses onto the cable scow, and John Hite took us across. His missus, he said, was making us supper. His son Homer ran the general store and post office.

Hite City turned out to be no more than a settlement with a couple dozen squat cabins and other structures thrown together with drift logs and chinked with mud. The roofs were made of thatch. Shade ramadas here and there offered relief from the sun.

The Hites had a stable of sorts for our horses. The hay came from a place called Fruita on the Fremont River, wherever that was. The mail came on horseback a hundred miles from the railroad at Green River, Utah. Hite was the supply hub for the gold mining operations downriver—placers and that big dredge, the *Hoskininni*.

John and his wife were around the marshal's age. John said his brother Cass was coming to town for his mail. They were expecting him for supper. "Big brother lives twelve miles downriver, in Glen Canyon, prettiest place you ever saw. 'Tickaboo,' he calls it."

"Tick-a-boo," Till repeated.

"In his younger days," John went on, "Cass prospected from British Columbia down into Mexico. Until him, nobody was even looking in these deserts. It was Hoskininni himself, the Navajo chief, who told him there was gold in Glen Canyon. Cass discovered this dandy

166

crossing and found gold here. He staked claim to nearly every crick mouth in the whole canyon. Speak of the devil, here he comes."

We looked downriver where John was pointing and saw a silver-haired man at the oars of a rowboat, pulling upstream in an eddy. Above him, some ravens were playing in the wind and croaking his arrival. Twelve miles upstream, for his mail and some company!

There were seven at Ma Hite's table that evening—the four Hites and the three of us. John slaughtered a couple of his wife's chickens for the occasion. The rest of her fare was fresh vegetables from their garden and the last of their watermelons.

Cass Hite, the old-timer, was tall and slender and walked somewhat stooped. His hair was thick and silver, his goatee white as salt. Cass proved even more loquacious than his brother and friendly as can be. He was hugely interested in the marshal's mission. They all were.

In the glow of their kerosene lamps, supper commenced with a prayer led by the elder brother, followed by compliments over the spread. John's wife must've had a name but I never learned it. Even her husband called her "Ma." Over supper the Hites passed around the marshal's photograph of the Fort Worth Five, and thought it sensational. All five of the outlaws had passed through Hite City over the years, always using aliases. "So that's

Butch Cassidy! So that's the Sundance Kid!" Homer and John allowed they'd suspected as much of those particular drifters.

All but the old man had seen Harvey Logan that morning. Logan stayed only half an hour before he rode out on the road to Hanksville, leading Peaches. Old Cass was amused that the marshal of Telluride had come all this way to recover a mule being delivered to Butch Cassidy.

"The boys are after their mule," the marshal said. "I'm after Logan, also known as Kid Curry." He explained that our thief killed a Wyoming sheriff in the aftermath of a train robbery.

The old man's grimace was filled with contempt. "And I always heard that Butch and his Wild Bunch ain't killers."

The marshal shrugged. "That's Butch's reputation. They say he shoots the horse lest he kill the rider. He won't even let his gang rob the train passengers—it's the safe in the express car he's after. But Harvey Logan's a different animal. He's lower than a snake's belly in a wagon rut."

"I'll second that," I put in, and described my encounter with Logan the night he stole Hercules and Peaches. At the last I said, "I believe he came within a hair of pulling the trigger."

Till shot me a look I couldn't quite decipher. Disbelief

with a touch of respect, I suppose. Back home I hadn't told how bad it actually was.

At this point, Homer—Cass's nephew—took a break from shoveling supper. "Charles Siringo came through here a year ago June."

"The Pinkerton detective," explained Till.

"That's him," said Homer. "You're a sharp one."

"Oh, yeah," I agreed.

Homer reached for the marshal's photo of the Fort Worth Five, which had landed in the center of the table. "Siringo was on the trail of three men who spent a fifty-dollar bill at the store in Hanksville. The serial number showed it came from that train robbery in Wyoming."

"I got a close look at the three when I ferried them across," John said. "That was two days before the Pinkerton man showed up. I believe all three are in this picture. One of 'em was this Harvey Logan—chewed tobacco then and this morning. This one standing up and this one sitting down were with him. What's their names?"

"Will Carver and Ben Kilpatrick," replied the marshal.

"Which of the five have bounties on their heads, and how much?"

"Ten thousand apiece on Cassidy and Longabaugh, eight thousand on Logan."

"I'm getting confused," said Ma Hite. "Name all of

them one by one if you would, marshal."

"Yes, ma'am. Sitting left to right, that's Sundance, Ben Kilpatrick, and Butch. Standing behind, that's Will Carver on the left and Harvey Logan on the right."

"Three have mustaches, but they're all clean-shaven. Derby hats and suits, what dandies they are! Who would've thought?"

"Logan growed out his beard since the picture was took," John said. "Today was the first I ferried any of 'em across this year."

"They keep on the move, usually split up," the marshal said. "For eleven years now—ever since Telluride—Butch spent most of the year in the saddle between Wyoming and the Gila Mountains way down in New Mexico. Works for a spell at different ranches, uses three or four different names."

"How'd you know about that?"

"From Charlie Siringo, in my office a couple years back. When the gang travels by train, they're on a spree, duded up and off to spend their loot. They've been traced to San Antonio and New Orleans, and Sundance goes back east, where he's from. Siringo has even tracked Butch and Sundance to New York City. Right now I expect they're at the Roost—maybe only Butch is. Back in Monticello we heard he's waiting on Peaches."

"Foolishness!" exclaimed Ma Hite. "What a petty man, what ornery toads they all are! You can't tell me they don't have blood on their hands."

Old Cass raised his eyebrows and pursed his lips. "What I'm wonderin', marshal, is whether you intend to keep up the pursuit."

"I'll track Logan all the way to the Roost if need be."

"Marshal," said John, "I don't like your chances of locating the Roost. It's not the one Butch had to abandon some years back, when the word got out. Seems two sisters with a ranch were keeping him supplied with beef and horses."

Cass nodded thoughtfully. "The hideout he's been using since then must be even more remote."

John took up where Cass left off. "It's got to be somewhere in that maze of badlands in the San Rafael Desert, but that's an enormous country. Logan is likely to stop at Charlie Gibbons's store in Hanksville, like they often do, but from there on nobody including the Pinkerton has ever been able to follow. Siringo thinks they tie buckskin bags or suchlike around the feet of their horses."

"Interesting," said the marshal, "but I've put a lot of thought into this. Robbers Roost, whatever it is, must have considerable water and sufficient graze for their horses. Can't be but a few such places in that desert. Maybe there's only one."

"And I know where it is," announced Cass Hite.

The old man's relatives were all ears and so were we. "Leastwise I'm pretty dern sure," Cass added. "Some people never forget a face. I never forget a place."

"You got my attention," the marshal said. "You been there?"

"That's what I'm sayin'."

"How long ago?"

"Early '80s. I was prospecting the San Rafael country. Stumbled across such a place as I was about to die of thirst. That's so powerful a spring, it's got a pool maybe thirty feet long. The creek that began there flowed a good half mile toward the Muddy River before it went underground."

Till's brow was furrowed. "The Roost ain't high up?"

"No, son, if that be Robbers Roost, it's in a shallow canyon."

"I always pitchered you had to climb up to it. A roost is something you perch on. Pass the dumplin's, please. Thanks for the vittles, ma'am—your gravy is boldacious."

"Why, thank you, Till. Say, Marshal Clark, I can't help but wonder why you haven't brought along a posse."

"I have," the marshal said. "Ma'am, you're lookin' at 'em." He pointed his fork at Till. "This one said, 'We'll be your posse.' I took him at his word."

"And now you propose to lead these boys all the way to Robbers Roost? What's that gonna look like? A hail of bullets?"

"Not necessarily," replied the marshal. "Like we've been saying, Butch is no killer."

"But Logan is."

"Which is why Butch Cassidy would agree to a swap. I get Logan and eight thousand dollars' bounty, and Butch gets to go free. I might even ride in there under a bonnet, wearin' a skirt and singin' 'Sweet Betsy from Pike.' What's Butch gonna do?"

Old Cass stroked his goatee gleefully. "Might work, might work."

Ma Hite harrumphed. "More foolishness!"

"Why are you so sure," put in John, "that Butch will hand Harvey Logan over?"

The marshal hesitated. "My strategy and the outcome will depend on circumstances. At the least, I intend to recover the mule and have a talk with Butch. I might leave it at that."

"And what would you tell Butch?" inquired Ma Hite.

"That his game is up."

"If you manage to ride into the Roost," the old man said, "that'll speak for itself. Butch would leave and never come back, and that would suit me just fine. He's put all of us in a bad light."

"Us?" his brother asked him.

"Every Mormon in Utah! I'm sick and tired of it!"

Ma Hite got up and started clearing the dishes. Till was squirming in his seat. "Hon, hang on for the watermelon," she told him.

Clark seemed agitated. He turned his gaze to the far end of the table. "In all that mess of canyons, Cass, we'd

173

never locate the Roost without you. I'd be mighty obliged if you would guide us."

The old-timer had to think about it. "Well, I shoulda seen that comin'. Now it's a case of put up or shut up. Guide you? Reckon I will."

23

THE MOMENT OF DECISION

AS THE OLD man led us out of Hite, my conscience was feeling better. I'd sent Ma a letter out of Homer's post office. It went like this:

> *October 11, 1900*
> *Hello Ma,*
> *I hope you can make out the postmark. Till and I are in Hite City, Utah, on the Colorado River in pursuit of Peaches with Telluride's marshal, Jim Clark. Hite City is something less than a metropolis. I am enamored of the redrock country and so is Till. Both of us are hale and hearty. The extra funds you sent came in*

handy for supplies. Will send a telegram from Telluride
when we get back. Then home!
   Affectionately, with tales to tell, Owen

I was under the impression that Hanksville was just up the road, but it turned out to be something like sixty miles. As monotonous and dusty as those nine hours were, they felt like forever. Somewhere off to our right ran the Dirty Devil River but I never spied it. Hanksville wasn't much to look at, dry and windy and so sand-blown that we rode into town with bandannas pulled over our noses like bandits. The storekeeper's eyes went big as quarters when he saw the marshal's badge.

Charlie Gibbons was a nervous little fellow. He puzzled over the marshal's photo, or pretended to. "You don't recognize these men?" Clark asked gruffly.

"Well, I do, but I've never seen them together, just one or two at a time, and never had an idea who they were. I've been told that Butch and his bunch do business here, but I always figured the less curious I was, the healthier."

The marshal pointed out Logan. "Seen this one recently, like yesterday or today? We tracked him here."

Gibbons shook his head. "Maybe passed through in the night?"

Outside of Hanksville the Fremont and the Muddy joined and became the Dirty Devil. We left the road,

176

which was headed north to the town of Green River. "There's no road where we're going," Cass announced. He steered us northwest up the Muddy River, which was sure enough muddy but more of a creek.

From where we camped on the chalky, wide-open plain, the cliffs of the San Rafael Reef loomed large. The big waterhole that might be Robbers Roost, to the best of Cass's recollection, was in one of the Muddy River's maze of side canyons between the San Rafael Reef and the San Rafael Swell.

The wind kicked up as we were collecting bits of driftwood and got worse as the marshal was heating up a big can of stew from Homer's store. In a second pot Cass was boiling water. The old man led us off a ways to find some Mormon tea. It grew in a clump, all stems and no leaves. We were breaking some off, when, with a glance toward camp, he said, "Twenty-eight thousand dollars is a small fortune."

I was at a loss but Till wasn't. "I added it up myself. That's the bounty for Butch and Sundance and Harvey Logan."

"You boys have been with the marshal a good while. You reckon there's gonna be gunplay?"

I hesitated. Not so, Till. "We know Butch is waitin' on Logan, but maybe Sundance and the other two ain't there. Maybe they is and maybe they ain't. The marshal's gonna shoot it out with Logan for killin' a sheriff. Takin' him alive ain't practical."

"Hmm . . ." said the old prospector. "What do you think, Owen?"

"Clark's more unpredictable than the weather around here."

Back at camp, Cass took the boiling water off the fire and set it aside. We threw in a couple handfuls of the wild tea and let it steep.

Come time to eat, the wind was blowing a sandy gale. You had to lift your bandanna clear of your mouth for every bite. We sopped chunks of Ma Hite's bread in the stew and drank the amber-colored tea. Till liked it so much, Cass warned him to ease up lest he be awake all night.

Clouds raced in and the temperature plummeted. After that, around dark, the wind quit but it stayed cold. Last thing before I fell asleep, Till was asking, "You reckon the marshal really brought along a bonnet and a skirt?"

We made an early start, everybody except Jim Clark wearing their coats. The marshal led out with his star showing and his gun belt bristling with cartridges. Till and I followed in our usual order and Cass Hite rode sweep. Before long we were riding four abreast across the plain of baked mud with cracks running every which way.

When we picked up the tracks of a horse and a mule, it was all but certain we were on Logan's trail. Before long we came across some old horse apples, and doubts set in. Maybe the tracks, like the droppings, weren't recent.

Over the eons, the Muddy River had carved a break in the San Rafael Reef. As we passed through the Reef we rode single file with old Cass in the lead. It took some maneuvering for Cass to lead his horse through a cluster of gigantic, sharp-edged blocks of sandstone fallen from the towering cliffs. There were no more prints to be seen of horses or mules. "Kid Curry put them foot bags on," Till said, and the marshal agreed.

Maybe half an hour later, where the canyon widened for a spell, Cass sang out, "Thar she blows!"

I flinched, thinking he'd spied the Roost, but that wasn't it. Cass was sitting easy in the saddle, signaling the rest of us to catch up. Fanning out beside him, we pondered some very fresh horse apples. "Practically steaming," the old-timer said.

"You'd think he would of used them big-city catch bags," the marshal said. "If they go to the trouble with the hoof bags, why not collect these telltale turds?"

Till had himself a good chortle. Cass said, "Logan's overconfident. Or just plain lazy."

The clouds were gone but the cold conditions remained. Jim Clark's weathered face was wearing a faint smile. The glare of the sun had him squinting, which deepened his crow's feet. What was he up to?

We soon came to a place where the creek had risen, then dropped, leaving patches of mud alongside. In the fresh mud were the deep and obvious imprints of the hoof bags. "Logan coulda walked 'em around here," Till said. "Don't have a lick of sense."

"It hasn't rained in days," I wondered aloud. "Yet the water's been up."

"Evidently it's been raining in the Wasatch Mountains," Cass explained. "They're a good long way upstream."

We drank from our canteens and dispatched the pastries Ma Hite had sent along. Ten minutes later we were back in the saddle.

The country was changing as we encountered an extremely hard layer of sandstone. The canyon of the Muddy narrowed, with reddish-tan cliffs on both sides. In addition there were frequent canyons coming in from our left and right. Those dry side canyons looked confusingly similar, all of them barren halls of stone. With our old prospector giving each of them a long look, it went without saying we were getting close.

Nobody was saying a word. Eventually Cass came to a side canyon he studied harder and longer than the others. It came in from our right. The old man was eyeballing a formation up above the canyon rim, a stranded remnant of a layer of stone all but eroded away. It was shaped like a turban, buff-colored with a band of red through the middle. Hite motioned us closer. "This be it," he whispered. "Don't say a word. Sound will carry in there like anything." I noticed the marshal take his badge off and put it in his pocket.

The side canyon we entered was bone dry. It narrowed between walls of a hundred feet or more. All of a sudden, from a ledge barely above our heads came an explosion of motion and sound. Till flinched, his eyes wide. I'd never been so spooked. Turns out we'd startled a great-horned owl. We watched it fly off down the canyon.

Maybe fifteen minutes later, those sheer walls shrank to fifty or so feet and stepped back on both sides. Up ahead on the dry creek bottom grew a lone cottonwood tree of considerable size, old and gnarled. Where we reached the tree, the streambed sand and gravels were conspicuously damp. No more than thirty yards on, we followed fresh tracks to the place the old man had remembered. Upstream, the creek was running on the surface. Right here, it went underground. Cass reined his horse around and signaled us to do the same. The four of us rode back to that big old cottonwood.

In the shade of the tree Cass dismounted and tethered his horse. The rest of us followed suit. "Let's parley," Hite whispered.

Keeping our eyes upstream, we drank from our canteens. More than a little agitated, Cass pulled on his goatish beard. "Now that we're here," he said, "I'm thinkin' I'm too old for the excitement. My ticker's tellin' me to go home."

The marshal was taken aback, but said, "Well, we thank you kindly. You sure this is the place you remembered?"

"Dead sure. I expect you'll find them roosting half a mile ahead."

Cass Hite mounted up and rode off. We watched the old-timer disappear around the bend. "Well, boys," Clark said, "we've reached the moment of decision."

"We can wait here, " I proposed, "while you—"

The marshal shook his head. "I can't shoot my way in there. My strategy depends on you two. If you're not up to it, we skedaddle right now."

As close to Clark as Till was standing, he had to look skyward to bring Clark's face into view. "Spill it, marshal."

"I'm gonna leave my weapons right here, even my knife. You'll go first, Till, with this on the end of a stick." Clark pulled a white handkerchief out of his vest pocket. "We're going in under a white flag."

Expecting something else, Till had a wrinkle of a smile. "Walkin' or ridin'?"

"Riding, in case we need to run for it, but we won't have to if you boys don't lose your nerve. We leave the packhorse here. We go in slow and peaceful and harmless. They ain't gonna start shooting."

"What about Harvey Logan?" I countered. "He's a killer."

"Not with three of us to kill and not in front of his

boss. Five minutes, you decide."

We took a short walk. Till said, "You want to get Peaches, don't you?"

"I'm good for it. I like the marshal's plan."

"Glad to hear it. If we turn around now, we're plumb yellow."

There was nothing left to do but smile. "Like Pa always said, it takes courage to be a Quaker."

24

THAT'S REALLY LOW

HOLDING UP THAT little white flag on a stick, Till led the way. Then me, holding my breath, then the marshal at the back of his so-called posse. Despite the chill, Clark still wasn't wearing his coat. It was rolled up behind his saddle so the outlaws could plainly see he had no gun belt.

Within minutes the stream was running strong and crystal clear, about three inches deep and twenty feet across. Till was keeping the colt's hooves in the water like Clark said. The canyon rims were diving and the view widening. Ahead, a cluster of leafy cottonwoods. Time was crawling but my heart was racing. I was looking to spot that big pool Cass Hite talked about. If I saw one, we were about to ride into a hornet's nest.

I was losing my nerve, but it was too late to turn back. All I could do was play my part and hope the marshal wasn't out of his mind.

There it was, the desert pool Cass remembered. Biting his lip hard enough to draw blood, Till rode up a beaten path around the pool. I heard angry voices on the wind. Moments later we were on a rise and looking down into the Roost. A raven was croaking. The breeze was stirring the yellowing leaves of the big cottonwoods. In the shade of the trees, three men seated on logs were playing cards and having an argument. Past them stood a crude cabin like the ones at Hite. Where was Peaches?

Till followed the trail through the water to their side of the creek. My heart was pounding its way out of my chest.

Till reined the colt in. We were out in the open, fifty, sixty feet away from the three men. One of them heard something and looked our way. His cards went flying as he drew his gun and leapt to his feet. A heartbeat later we were looking into the barrels of three revolvers. Till gave his white flag a little wave and croaked, "Howdy, fellers!"

They fanned out, crouching, getting a better look at us. "What the Sam Hill?" said the one on the left.

Just then, with the danger seemingly past, one of their .45s went off like a cannon. Till's horse reared and mine crow-hopped to the side. Till's white flag was on the ground—was he hit? The rogue who'd fired was the one on the right, with a beard. Harvey Logan, damn his hide. The one in the middle yelled, "Birdbrain, what'd you do that for?"

"Shot over their heads!"

"It's just us," the marshal called soothingly. He rode a bit closer, with Till and me on either side. What a relief to know all three of us were unscathed.

The outlaws were dressed like ranch hands and wore wide-brimmed slouch hats like mine. The trigger-happy louse with the beard was unmistakably Logan. I hadn't forgotten the rustler's cruel face. I recognized the man to the left—Harry Longabaugh, the Sundance Kid—from the marshal's photo. As to the leader in the middle, stalking ahead of the other two with his gun pointed at the marshal's chest, I'd met him in person and so had Till. Sandy hair, square jaw, piercing gray eyes. It was Butch Cassidy, the man we called Moneybags.

"Your guns ain't friendly," drawled the marshal while raising his hands. "I'm unarmed, as you can see, and so are these Quaker boys."

"Quaker boys?" echoed Cassidy with a glance our way.

"That's right, they wouldn't harm a fly. Don't you recognize me?"

"Why should I?" Butch snapped.

"What about your friends? What's their names?"

"What's it to you? Are you Charlie Siringo?"

"I'm Jim Clark. Come on, Butch, you remember."

Cassidy strode closer, gun up and cautious. "From Telluride," he said finally, and slowly holstered his revolver.

"Now you got it. San Miguel Valley Bank."

Cassidy's cohorts put down their guns, and I breathed easier.

Butch was still staring. "Telluride was a long time ago. You still the marshal?"

"Still am."

"Where's the badge?"

"In my pocket. Let's say I'm here in a 'unofficial capacity.'"

Cassidy broke into a grin. "I hear ya."

"We're saddle sore," the marshal said. "Yonder shade looks inviting."

Logan was giving me the evil eye, plainly wishing he'd left me for the vultures back at Hermosa Creek.

We'd barely sat down on the logs by their fire ring when Till came out with "What about us, Butch? Don't you reconnize us?"

"Don't call me Butch," Cassidy barked.

"Should I call you Bob, or Leroy?"

"Hey, wait a minute, you're the kid that kicked me in the shin!"

At this, Sundance hooted and slapped his knee.

"Pueblo train yards, that's right," Till said to Butch.

"You were being a bully."

Angry all over again, Cassidy turned his stare on me. "I made you a generous offer for your mules."

"We didn't want to sell," I said with a shrug. "I mentioned we were on our way to our new farm in Hermosa. My mistake, I guess."

The Sundance Kid looked perplexed. Logan spat a stream of tobacco juice.

Till said to Sundance, "What's *your* name?"

"Harry Alonzo."

"Harry Alonzo Longabaugh? Can I call you Sundance?"

Longabaugh laughed. "Call me what you please, little bugger. What's your handle?"

"I'm Till, and this is my brother, Owen. As I was about to explanate, Butch had Logan here steal Peaches."

"Steal your peaches?"

"Peaches is the name of our Appaloosa mule. Logan stole her and Hercules from our barn and drew down on Owen."

"Hmm," said Butch.

Harvey Logan wasn't saying anything.

Till was just getting started. "Owen tracked Logan all the way to Telluride in a bad snowstorm! Logan sold off Hercules to work in the mines."

"That's low," said Sundance, with a smirk in Butch's direction.

"In Telluride, Logan had a saddle made for Peaches.

It was all so Butch could have a new riding mule and get back at us."

"Butch loves pranks, but that's *really* low," Sundance said, smirking some more.

"Bunch of fiddle-faddle if you ask me," said Till.

It was about time I spoke up. "We reckon Peaches is here. We came to get her back."

Sundance slapped his knee. "Best story I heard in years. You always did have trouble taking no for an answer, Butch, but you *like* kids."

"Not these two." He hooked his thumb at Till. "Especially the whippersnapper."

"You boys have sure livened up the afternoon," Sundance said. "We don't get much company. So, if I get this straight, you've made the acquaintance of these two, but how'd you recognize me?"

"Easy," said Till. "From the marshal's photograph. It was taken in Fort Worth. Are Will Carver and Ben Kilpatrick here, too?"

Cassidy was peeved. "Clark, *you* got that picture? We're the only ones got that picture."

"You don't say," drawled the marshal. "I got one in my saddlebags. By now it must be plastered in every post office in the country."

Clark fetched it, and the desperadoes took a close look. Sundance said, "The joke's on us, Butch."

"This is stupid," growled Logan.

Butch turned on his errand boy. "They trailed you all

the way to the Roost. How'd that happen?"

"Give 'em a medal! It was bound to happen someday."

"You used the hoof bags?"

"Sure thing, Boss."

"And the catch bags?"

Logan's answer was a sneer. Till was enjoying this no end.

"I told you!" Cassidy thundered. "Always use the catch bags! Now what do we do?"

"My mistake. I'll take care of 'em for you, all three."

"Take care of 'em?"

"You know."

"No, I don't know. You're through, Logan. Grab your stuff and git."

The marshal added, "Just so you know, Harvey Logan—alias Kid Curry—the bounty on you is up to eight thousand."

Logan turned to Butch. "In that case I want more."

"More what?"

"More loot."

"You got plenty after the last job. So long and good luck."

"Not that direction," said the marshal, pointing downstream. "Unless I collect my packhorse first."

I exchanged glances with Till. Now was the time for Clark to announce he was taking Logan. But the marshal was unarmed, and didn't say a word.

"You heard him," Butch said to Logan. "Use the back

door. You got plenty of time to make yourself scarce before the marshal can send any telegrams."

Harvey Logan stomped off cursing a blue streak.

I was keen on seeing Peaches and said so. Till got up with me. To my surprise the Sundance Kid joined us. Leaving Butch and the marshal to catch up on old times, I supposed. As we passed by the cabin, Logan was collecting his stuff. He stood in the open door and gave us more dirty looks.

It was strange to be walking alongside an outlaw wearing a gun, but reassuring under the circumstances. Unlike Butch Cassidy, the Sundance Kid wore a ready smile. Sundance was watching out for us until their ex-partner was gone.

We passed the empty corral and then, after all this time, we finally laid eyes on Peaches. Along with three horses, she was hobbled and grazing in the grass up the creek. "Peaches!" Till called as we drew close.

Peaches whinnied in reply, and pointed those long ears our way. "Yep, it's us!" I cried. Peaches lifted her head and brayed. Pretty soon she was taking the scent of our hands and nuzzling us up and down and snorting. "We found you at last," Till told her. "And we're taking you home," I added.

Logan passed by without a word or glance. We watched him ride out. "Good riddance," Sundance muttered.

The three of us went and sat on the creek bank.

Peaches followed, keeping us close.

Butch's sidekick took his time rolling a smoke. It seemed like Sundance was somewhere else in his mind, tired and glum in equal measure. When he returned to the present, he said, "You boys got a lot of sand to come all this way."

"All the way from Kansas," Till replied, and went on. I was surprised to hear him telling about Pa dying. Till was finally accepting it. He soon changed the subject: "What's it like to be an outlaw?"

Sundance shook his head. "I wouldn't wish it on anybody. You start out small, and after a while it gets out of control."

"Like Butch stealing a pair of overalls?"

"You heard about that?"

"I read it in a book."

"What'd it say?"

"He was the oldest of eleven kids . . ."

"Close, it was thirteen."

"Well, he rode a long way into town, except the store was closed when he got there. So he broke in—"

"Let himself in. The way Butch tells it, the door was open."

"So, he took the overalls and left some kinda note. Said he'd come back and pay for 'em, but the owner got him arrested anyway."

"The district attorney decided not to prosecute, but Butch didn't let it go. Still resents it."

"What about you? How did you—"

"Me, I don't have an excuse. I'm what you might call temperamentally unsuited."

"Unsuited to what?"

Sundance laughed. "To making an honest living."

Till was vexed. "But really, how come?"

"It's not an honest game. The bigwigs expect you to slave for crumbs."

"You're a wanted man, right?"

"In seven states I know of. It gets old."

"But how will it end?"

The famous robber flicked his cigarette, unsmoked, into the creek. "¿*Quién sabe?* We passed the point of no return a long time ago. One thing's for sure—I ain't goin' back to prison."

With that, Sundance peeled off and disappeared around the bend, back toward Butch and the marshal. We lingered with Peaches maybe fifteen minutes. Suddenly, like an apparition from hell, Harvey Logan appeared from up the creek. He spurred his horse into a lope and was on us in no time. We looked over our shoulders, but there was no help in sight.

The reins were in his left hand. His right was at his hip, ready to draw his pistol. His features were hateful as ever and smug as can be. "Forgot something," he said with a grin.

"What's that?" Till retorted, his voice trembling yet defiant.

"To kill your stupid mule."

There was maybe thirty feet between that louse and us, and less than half that between him and Peaches. With a sneer on his lips, Logan drew and pointed his revolver at her head. Enjoying the moment, he paused to meet my eyes and mock me. "Like I said, it's your misfortune."

I felt utterly helpless. As Logan readied to shoot, his horse took a step or two. He had to wait before he could aim again, long enough for my mind to lurch and think of something. Was it still there? I slid my hand into the pocket of my mackinaw and took hold of that strange rock, round as a baseball. I reared back and let it fly.

No shot rang out. Logan fell from his horse to the ground, knocked out cold, or was he dead?

"You got him!" Till crowed. "Owen, you beaned him! What a throw!"

"Plumb lucky," I said.

We approached cautiously. It appeared I only grazed him. A gash above Logan's ear was bleeding. I knelt and put two fingers on his jugular. "Alive," I reported.

Till sprang for Logan's six-shooter where it had fallen, cocked it, and stood back, aiming with both hands. "Keep him covered," I said.

"You bet I will."

I undid Logan's bandanna from his neck and folded it into a long strip as neatly as my trembling hands allowed. I rigged it across his forehead and around his temples, and tied it tight at the base of his skull.

When Logan came to a few minutes later, we had him covered with his sidearm and rifle. He rode off dazed without either one.

25

WHERE WILL YOU GO?

BACK AT THE cabin, Butch and Sundance took Logan's weapons off our hands and listened with amusement to our story. "Good for you," they said, and "Serves him right."

When we caught up with the marshal, he was pulling his saddlebags off his horse. He seemed more annoyed than interested. "Are you gonna get after Logan?" Till ventured to ask. "Before he gets away? We'll split the bounty with ya."

"Quit your sass, he ain't worth the trouble. You boys go and collect the packhorse."

"Okay," I said reluctantly. The marshal was up to something, but what?

"Don't unpack him when you bring him back," Clark added. "We might not be staying. For the time being, hobble our horses with theirs so they can graze."

Till and I saddled up and rode down the creek to fetch the packhorse. We wondered why the marshal was undecided about roosting with Butch, his old buddy. The obvious answer came to us shortly. He didn't trust him.

Tethered to a low branch on that lone cottonwood, the marshal's packhorse snorted his disapproval. He'd been left in sight of water and a patch of grass without resort to either. We got off our horses and tied up. Till took a seat on a fallen limb. I told him I was going to walk the packhorse up to the running water for a drink. "Sounds good," he said. "Think I'll take a snooze."

When I got back Till was nowhere in sight. I fought the impulse to call out, and thought about where he might be. Then I knew: behind the rock slab where the marshal stashed his weapons.

Till was so preoccupied he didn't hear me coming. He was sitting cross-legged with the marshal's ivory-handled revolver in his lap, admiring its deadly perfection and making the cylinder go *click-click-click*. When he suddenly saw me, he looked up like a guilty thing surprised.

"Till," I said, none too pleased.

"This is Colt's Peacemaker," little brother said reverently, "the gun that won the West."

"It's big," I allowed. "Longer than Logan's."

Till nodded gravely. "Thirteen inches tip to butt."

I suggested he put it back in the marshal's gun belt, and he did. I guessed Till hadn't played with the rifle yet. It was lying there on a flat rock next to the pigsticker in its sheath.

Till said, "The marshal didn't say nothin' about his weapons. Should we bring 'em?"

I had to think about that. "He felt safer around the outlaws without them. We better leave it that way."

When we got back to the Roost, no one was around, not even up the creek where we took the horses. It appeared that Cassidy, Sundance, and Clark were off on a walk. Since when did the marshal go for walks?

"It's about plunder," Till declared. "That's why the marshal was gettin' his saddlebags. They got some loot hid somewhere, and they're gonna give him some."

"Till, you might've just hit the bull's-eye, and I can explain what that's about. Back in Telluride, people say that when Butch was making his getaway eleven years ago, he left a payoff for the marshal under a log."

"I remember Clark tellin' us he was out of town."

"Like he arranged with Butch! Here's what I'm thinking. Once the marshal found out how much Butch and the other two stole—more than twenty thousand, more than he guessed they would—he's been bent out of shape about it ever since. Whatever they left for him, he thought he deserved a bigger cut."

Till liked my line of speculation. "Maybe a quarter share, like a equal partner. That's what he's been after all this time, ever since we left Telluride. We're onto him, Owen!"

"Maybe from the first, way back in his office, the marshal was thinking of us as a ploy to get into the Roost. Even the white flag! Maybe this whole trip was never about chasing a rustler or collecting a bounty like he told the Hites, or getting Peaches back. Clark knew that Logan was headed for the Roost to hand off Peaches, and what he really was after was this meet-up with Butch that he's having right now."

"Which explanates why he never tried very hard to catch up with Logan."

"He played us like fish, Till."

"Like sapheads! Like chumps! Hey, what if Butch and Sundance don't wanna share? They're packin' guns and he ain't."

The country surrounding the Roost was smooth, solid rock—slickrock, as it's called—and there was no telling where they'd gone. Somewhere out there, in some crevice, Butch Cassidy had a cache of plunder.

It wasn't long before they came walking in, all three with saddlebags over their shoulders. Butch and Sundance eased theirs down, bulging and heavy, so full the flap straps barely reached the buckles. Canvas was showing in the gaps. The marshal's bags weren't quite as full. They made clinking metallic sounds as he set them down.

It didn't take much imagination to figure out what

was doing the clinking: high-denomination gold coins.

Butch and the marshal were straight-faced, but a smile was playing on the lips of the Sundance Kid. He was plenty sturdy, a bit taller than Butch and wider across the shoulders, but his features were pleasant by nature. You wouldn't take him for a gunman and a robber.

"You two got the packhorse?" the marshal barked at us, ugly as can be.

"We got him," I said.

"Packed and ready?"

"Still packed."

"Brought my guns?"

I hesitated. "You didn't say to."

"Are they still where I put 'em?"

I knew he wouldn't want me to say the real reason I left them, not in front of Butch and Sundance. I said, "We didn't look."

Clark exploded. "How do I know they're still there?"

We'd never seen him like this. Till and I exchanged glances and Butch and Sundance did the same. The marshal was all red in the face, vein-popping enraged.

"No need to be slantindicular," Till told him.

"Slantindicular!" he stormed. "What's that, kid?"

Till made a silly face. "Beats me."

The marshal lunged at him with that huge right hand. "I oughta wring your neck!"

The Sundance Kid grasped the marshal's wrist, and

200

the marshal shook him off. "I'm leaving," Clark told the outlaws. To us he said, "You two are on your own."

Till stuck out his jaw. "Suits me."

The marshal stared at me long and hard. "On second thought, get your mule and be quick about it."

I considered the menace in his eye. Now that he'd revealed himself a volcano, I was plumb scared of sticking with him. It was obvious we knew what was in his saddlebags. I said, "We'll bring your horses back to Telluride, but we'd rather poke around by ourselves."

"Poke around doing what?"

I had no idea. "Looking for fossils," I heard myself saying.

"Stupidest thing I ever heard. You'll starve out or break your necks. You're coming with me."

Watching all this while, Butch up and said, "No they ain't, Clark, and that's that."

The marshal scowled. "Have it your way. I could care less."

A short while later the four of us watched Clark ride out down the creek, trailing his packhorse. "Owen, you done good," Sundance said.

"I'll second that," Butch chimed in. "Both of you," he added, with a nod in Till's direction.

Till tipped his hat. "Thanks for the cover, Butch."

That evening they roasted what they had left of a desert bighorn. We sat on those logs at right angles back from the fire, the famous outlaws on one, Till and I on the other. Their faces in the firelight made a picture to remember.

"Our last night at the Roost," Butch was saying. He didn't seem the sentimental sort but his voice was unmistakably wistful.

"How come is that?" Till asked.

"Well, kid, we been chased all over the West, lawmen every which way, bullets flying, so many close scrapes, but we always had the Roost. If there was ever gonna be a sign, today was it. Our time is up."

"We pushed our luck and then some," Sundance agreed.

"The telegraph was one thing, but it won't be long before they can telephone from town to town."

Sundance chuckled. "A recent railroad job we did, they had a horse car all ready for us. Threw upon a door and mounted men rode out, rifles blazing!"

Butch poked his pal in the ribs. "Think about it this way, pardner. They finally ran down Geronimo but we're still free. If we're gonna have the last laugh, it's time to throw in our cards and leave the table."

"It was bound to come," said Sundance. "I feel relieved, to tell you the truth."

"Where will you go?" I asked them. "I mean, what will you do?"

Butch shrugged. "Good questions. With that Fort

Worth picture everywhere, we might have to leave the country."

"Canada, maybe?"

"Too cold, and the Mounties are too good. We wouldn't last a month."

"Mexico?"

"Already got chased around there, same as Geronimo."

"South America!" Till cried. In a blur, he jumped up and ran over to where we'd pitched our tarp.

Butch watched him go. "The snapper's growin' on me. You never know what to expect."

Sundance laughed. "He might be onto something. In South America nobody would know us from Adam."

Till came back to the firelight with our *National Geographic*. He was all lit up. "There's this article in here called 'Road to Bolivia.' Tells about Argentina, too!" He handed it to Butch. "You can keep it."

"Okay, I will." Cassidy chuckled as he took the magazine in hand. "We'll look into it. You keep that mule saddle, okay?"

Till was all smiles. "Gee whillikers, it's a deal. It'll remind us how much you admirated Peaches."

"After all my years on horseback, I was ready to try a mule. Heard they ride better and can't be beat in rough country. Talk about footing . . . supposedly their vision includes their back feet as they're looking ahead."

"Kit Carson always rode a mule," Till informed him.

"Why, there you go. As it turns out, it was late in the game to be trying a new trick."

"I reckon I'll ride Peaches from here on. I can trail the marshal's colt if you got a halter rope."

Butch grinned. "We got a halter rope and some grub, too, if you don't mind eatin' out of tin cans."

"We're good at that" was Till's reply. "I reckon we'll be pullin' out in the morning."

Sundance had something on his mind. "Which way you boys headed?"

I said, "The way we came, I suppose."

He shook his head. "The marshal's likely camped just down the creek. He's got no further use for you two, and you know too much. That man's got more sins on his head than everybody who's rode with the Wild Bunch, combined."

"So, which way do we go?"

"Out the back door with us. We'll show you the way."

26

SPELLBOUND

WE RODE NORTH with the outlaws, out their "back door" as they called it, into a vast desert wilderness of bare rock in monumental shapes that beggar description. They were going to show us the best way to get back to Telluride.

It wasn't but an hour before Sundance held up, pointing, and said, "We're going thisaway, and you need to go thataway." Our destination, as he explained, lay to the northeast. The town of Green River was sixty or seventy miles away, on the Denver and Rio Grande Railroad. We could put our animals on the train there, eastbound. "Make sure you go with them," Sundance joked.

"And don't forget to change trains at Grand Junction," Butch added, "or you'll end up in Denver."

I had a feeling they were making this sound easier than it might turn out to be.

"We like to steer by the North Star," Sundance suggested. "You know where it's at?"

"In the north," Till answered. "Pa showed us."

Butch pointed out the San Rafael Reef to our right. "You crossed through the Reef yesterday when you came up the Muddy. Looked like a line of cliffs running north to forever. From this side it looks like a ridge. Keep a few miles clear of it, just keep following the ridge north until you strike the railroad. Follow the tracks east and you're at Green River."

We thanked them kindly and were about to say goodbye. Till was watering up. "You should come see us at Hermosa someday."

Butch looked doubtful. Sundance said, "*¿Quién sabe? Hasta la vista, amigos.*"

Till had the last word. "So long, fellers. Gosh all fish hooks!"

They went their way and we went ours, trying to keep them in sight as long as we could: Butch Cassidy and the Sundance Kid, armed with their Colts and Winchesters, saddlebags full of plunder, riding into the far distance. From one moment to the next, they disappeared into the folds of the land.

We rode on, keeping the Reef to our right, into a world

too fanciful to be real. We clattered across slickrock terraces and rode over sand dunes turned to stone. I was taken by all of it, spellbound by the immensity of time. I was keeping my eye out for the Morrison formation, and had a pretty good idea what it would look like. Late the night before, I built up the fire and found what I was looking for in *Behold the Dinosaur*: the illustration of all the rock layers of the Colorado Plateau, like a tall stack of building blocks. Fairly high up, among the younger layers, it showed the Morrison formation atop the San Rafael Group. Where the two met it said PRIME DINOSAUR HUNTING.

Here I was in the San Rafael Desert, in a place where maybe nobody had searched. I was looking for greenish or reddish bands of mudstones and siltstones. The dinosaurs lay buried in remnants of meandering streambeds.

The cold weather had passed through and it was warming up fast. About an hour after we said goodbye to our outlaws, I spied a promontory off to our left with bands of various colors. It resembled a colossal ship coming at us head-on. "That's gotta be the Morrison!" I cried.

Till doffed his hat and scratched. "What the heck's the Morrison?"

Little brother thought I was nuts when I insisted we go over there. "It's miles out of our way! How much water you think we got?"

"Not much, but if I find a dinosaur, I'll die happy."

"I won't. Your chances stink."

"I know. Give me one hour."

"Starting now?"

"Starting once we get there!"

It took longer than I guessed to reach my ship-like promontory. Its hues included green, purple, gray, tan, and maroon. Unfortunately, its slopes were too steep to climb. Only along its base could I get a close look, to the right of its blunt prow or to the left.

I went right. Till borrowed Pa's pocket watch and went left.

Studying that rock face took more concentration than I'd summoned in my life. I was looking for a pattern, anything that might be a fossil bone.

I had covered maybe eighty yards when Till appeared at my elbow wearing a triumphant grin. On his outstretched palm was an agatized shark's tooth nearly three inches long. "Your hour's up!"

"Lucky kid, where'd you find that?"

"On the ground, where else?"

I hadn't been looking on the ground.

"Let's get going, Owen!"

"Gimme that watch."

He handed it over. "Half an hour," I said. "Why don't you visit with Peaches or take a nap? Better yet, go back to your side and find me a dinosaur!"

Till was disgruntled, but at least he was gone. I redoubled my efforts, studying the ground as well as the slope.

Time was running out and my vision was swimming.

At last I spotted something about nine feet up, a pattern my mind detected as my eyes were moving on. I looked again and locked onto a telltale shape embedded in a gray background: a brownish, curving, bladelike tooth. How I wished I could get closer.

"Eureka!" I hollered, so loud Till came running.

"What is it?" he yelled.

He arrived at my side all out of breath. I pointed. "My dinosaur, Till, up there!"

"I don't see no dinosaur."

"The tooth of one—as long as my middle finger—right there! The tooth of a huge meat eater!"

Till squinted. "Good job, Owen. Lucky for us he's good and dead."

I was beside myself. Was the rest of the dinosaur hidden in the rock, waiting to be excavated? Its dimensions must be enormous. Was this another *Allosaurus*, the carnivore Arthur Lakes discovered, or something different? Every cell in my body was buzzing.

"Off we go," sang Till.

I thought about marking the spot with a rock cairn but realized that would be the height of folly. I just had to fix everything about this place in my memory so I'd be able to find it again. On we rode with me craning my neck to make a mental picture of the promontory and surrounding landscape.

The day turned into a scorcher. By midafternoon we

were sharing our spare canteen. How long could the animals last? As for forage, there wasn't any.

We rode a long, long way, keeping a couple miles off the Reef like Butch had said. The sun was close to setting and we were about to camp in a dry wash with nothing to recommend it.

Like us, the horses were glassy-eyed and resigned. Not so, Peaches. Till was about to unsaddle her but she didn't like the idea. Her eyes were alert and her nostrils quivering. She bobbed her head, blew a couple times, and whinnied for good measure. "Smells water," said Till.

Rather than camp, we continued down the stony wash as it cut through the Reef. We were going off course, but that mattered little compared to finding water. Till could barely hold Peaches back. She led us to a spring on the cliffy side of the Reef where the view opened up far and wide. The water trickled from a long, fern-decorated seam between a thin band of shale and the surrounding sandstone. The flow collected in a series of deep stone potholes. We and the animals drank our fill.

We pitched our tarp at the base of a colossal, sharp-edged slab of red sandstone maybe forty feet high that had fallen from the cliffs. Its nearly vertical face was rippled with wavy parallel lines. I took it for petrified mud, an ancient creek bottom. To my surprise I recognized improbably large birdlike tracks in the mud turned to stone. "Look, Till, a dinosaur walked through our camp!"

He craned his neck. "Reckon it was missing a tooth?"

We talked about our route and figured there was no need to backtrack. As the Reef marched north, we could follow it on its east side as well as its west.

From our campsite, as we were eating some canned salmon, we spied a freight wagon in the distance. It was pulled by a team of six mules and was headed south, with supplies for Hanksville and Hite City as we got to figuring. Where we'd left the road outside of Hanksville, Cass said it was headed north to Green River.

Our detour had not only delivered water but a road to follow. Green River, here we come!

27

HOMEWARD BOUND

IN GREEN RIVER we stabled Peaches and the marshal's horses, and stayed at a nearby hotel. It rained all night, and it was raining when we changed trains in Grand Junction, Colorado. We spent another night in a hotel in Montrose. From Ridgway, where we boarded the Rio Grande Southern, the San Juans were something to see. The rains had fallen as heavy snow on the jagged string of peaks that included Mount Sneffels. In full sun they shone brilliantly white. I was thinking about Molly and hoping to see her and Merlin Custard.

We pulled into Telluride around 2:00 p.m. There was

a train leaving for Durango at 2:35 we might catch if we were lucky. Till ran into the depot to buy tickets while I led the buckskin and the colt down the tracks, headed for the marshal's stable.

The kid working there was about as curious as the post he was leaning on. He had no idea who I was or where I'd been with the town's horses. He mentioned that the marshal was away but didn't know where. I didn't fill him in. I grabbed our bedrolls and such off the horses, threw them in a grain sack, and took off running.

Nearing the depot, I made a beeline across the street to the bakery. I was out of breath as I came through the door. Just like the first time, there was nobody there but Molly and me. "Owen!" she cried. "You're back!"

First thing, Molly took me out the door and onto the street. "I've been seeing Hercules! They're not keeping him up at the Tomboy. They rented him to Rogers Brothers. He overnights in town and goes up and back every day."

Till showed up, and the three of us flew down the street toward a long line of mules—on their own, with empty pannier bags—on their way back from the mines. "Got tickets for us and Peaches for the two thirty-five to Durango," Till panted. "We might make it!"

Lo and behold, there was Hercules, headed for the stables. I could've cried.

Seconds later the big fellow was shaking his ears at us as I hurried to free his halter rope from the pack frame. Quick as we might, we stuffed everything from the grain sack into his panniers. We started running and Hercules broke into a trot.

Molly was at my side as I raced down the tracks with Hercules. Till veered off to collect Peaches from behind the depot. "Buy a ticket for Hercules!" I yelled after him. A few minutes later we were all together at trackside. Hercules and Peaches nuzzled and snorted, reunited at last. I kept looking to see if anybody was after me for grabbing Hercules. If they tried to stop me I would . . . I didn't know what I was going to do, only that I was taking him and that was that.

Till held up our tickets for the conductor. The conductor called down the line to the man at the stock car, who was about to go up the gangplanks and close the door. I said we would stick with our mules. "Suit yourself," said the conductor.

Down to the stock car we hustled. The engineer blew the warning whistle.

Till went up the planks with Peaches. I was about to follow with Hercules but turned to face Molly.

"Write," she told me.

"Count on it," I promised. I looked into her eyes and didn't know what to say. I kissed her instead, which surprised her and me both.

"See you," I said.

Molly was beaming. "Hope so, Owen!"

I went up and into the car with Hercules and handed him off to Till. I remembered something I was dying to tell Molly and turned around in time. She was still there. "Saw a dinosaur tooth in the rock!" I called with fingers far apart. Molly gave a cheer as the door was closing.

The whistle screeched and the train lurched into motion. It had all happened so fast, Hercules was still harnessed, packsaddle and pannier bags and all. After the value beyond reckoning the Tomboy got out of our stolen mule, I wasn't going to lose sleep over a cheap pack outfit. As to ownership of Hercules, I doubted they would argue it after they talked with the train people and figured out it was me who took him. They knew he was mine and would lose any attempt to prove otherwise.

Cresting Lizard Head Pass, I was already thinking about spring thaw, and pulling stumps and rocks out of the field with mule power. I saw myself harnessing Hercules and Peaches to the riding plow, taking the seat, reins in hand and calling, "Let's go! Let's go!"

Late afternoon, our train pulled into Durango. I'd been gone three weeks but it felt like a whole lot longer. Eleven miles to go. Till rode Peaches on the fancy new saddle and I walked the big fellow by his halter rope. We were wearing our mackinaws against the chill of the evening. "Well, brother," I said, "it took some doing but we pulled it off. We're bringing both of them home safe and sound."

"Yes sir. I was just thinkin' the same thing. With only one shot fired!"

"You ain't disappointed?" I asked with a grin.

Till laughed. "Not hardly."

It was all but dark as we turned into the lane that led to Trimble Hot Springs. Ominously, the air was pungent with a burnt smell. Minutes later we learned why as we spied the eerie silhouette of a ruin where Trimble's elegant hotel had stood. The nearby buildings had also burned down, but the stables were still standing.

No one was around. Knowing Ma had been staying in one of the cottages, we feared the worst. I was queasy all over. We stopped up the road at the nearest house and I asked about the fire. "Somebody knocked over a lamp, was what I heard," the man told us. "Three days ago."

Till was on the verge of tears. "Our ma worked at the hotel."

"Don't worry, boys. Nobody got hurt."

What a relief that was. What would have become of us? With only a mile to go, we headed for home. When we turned into the driveway and saw light in the windows, I was overcome.

"Ma, we're home!" Till hollered as we drew close. "We're home!"

Ma came out on the porch with a lamp, and when she saw us with Hercules and Peaches in hand, she cried for joy, loud enough that Queenie nickered from the barn. "Thank God, Ma," I said. "The Trimble fire . . . where were you when it broke out?"

"In my cottage, late in the evening. I saw the flames from my window. We got everybody out in time."

The three of us gushed some more, nothing that was making much sense. I broke off to take care of Hercules and Peaches. I could see how ready they were for the barn and a long drink and fresh hay.

Minutes later, on my way into the house, I heard Till saying, "Owen beaned an outlaw with this rock!"

"Beaned an outlaw?"

"A bad outlaw, the one that stole Hercules and Peaches."

"*Beaned* him, what does that mean?"

"Hit him in the head!"

"Hmm," Ma said, looking my way as I hung up my mackinaw. "Let's talk about that later. I've been worried about my boys, and I'm so relieved you're back."

Till was so tuckered out, his head nearly hit the table while we were having bread and jam with milk, and apples and cheese. The kid stumbled to his couch and was asleep in seconds, my purple rock in hand. I hadn't known he retrieved it back at the Roost. If he wanted to keep it, that was okay by me. Its luster as a geological specimen was gone.

217

Ma and I kept the lamp burning awhile. As I gave her a short history of my time away, Ma's eyebrows rose on a number of occasions. I had some explaining to do. I was somewhat in the doghouse.

28

FINE AS A FROG HAIR

ANXIOUS TO REUNITE with his squirrel gun, Till bolted from the breakfast table. Ma seized the occasion to let me know that shortly after I left, she took out a loan for $3,000 so we could stay above water. It was due in three years, with our land and improvements as collateral, including the house, the barn, the well, even the privy. I was taken aback but didn't say so. This was going to take time to digest, and I had a very bad feeling about it. How likely was it we could make enough to pay it back?

I set that worry aside in favor of freeing our animals from their stalls and turning them loose to the pasture. Inside the barn I had some work to do. The night before,

I hadn't unpacked the panniers I took off Hercules. I went to pulling bedrolls, rain slickers, and such out of the canvas bags. Lifting the first bag, apparently empty, I realized it wasn't. There was something heavy at the bottom.

I got the surprise of my life. Reaching in, I pulled out a shiny bar of gold bullion.

My impulse was to shout to high heaven for Till to come see, but I stifled it. I couldn't believe what I was holding in my hand. Solid gold! I had an idea what a standard ingot of bullion looked like. This one was half as thick, not that I was complaining.

The thing was so heavy, it took both hands to hold it very long. I turned it over, looking for an imprint, something like PROPERTY OF THE TOMBOY MINE.

The bar was smooth as a baby's bottom—not a word, number, or mark of any kind.

Wait a minute, I thought, and went to pulling our stuff from the second pannier. Lo and behold, here was another shiny gold bar, an identical twin.

In a flash I weighed one of them on our scales. Fourteen pounds exactly. I set them on a stool, sat down on a bale of hay, and had myself a good think. After I left town with the marshal, the Tomboy rented Hercules out. He'd been making the daily trip from town up to the mine loaded down with supplies, sixteen mules to a packer, and making the trip back to town on his own.

Gold bullion from the Tomboy, hidden at the bottom

of his panniers? What was that about?

Something Merlin had said came to mind. The Tomboy not only had its own mill onsite, they had recently added a retort. In small amounts, they would soon be refining their gold concentrates into bullion. Were these the first ingots they cast, without identifying words or numbers?

The questions kept coming. Why hide the ingots on one of the mules meandering by themselves back to town? Why not transport the bullion with armed men?

Robbers and bloodshed, that's what they were afraid of. Safer to sneak the gold into town. Given the size and shape of the bars, the panniers on their bullion mule would appear to be empty. Who would ever imagine a scheme like that? Even if somebody were to guess the secret, they would have to search many dozens of mules plodding the length of that six-mile trail.

When the Tomboy chose Hercules for the task, they hadn't given a thought to me. Nobody in or around Telluride had seen me in ten or more days. They thought I gave up and went home.

All of a sudden I heard footsteps and nearly jumped out of my skin. Not to worry, it was Ma. When she saw what was on that stool, her eyebrows arched up like inchworms.

I had a lot to explain, and Ma listened with rapt attention. Every now and again we heard the crack from Till's .22. The shots sounded far off, way down by the river.

That was a good thing. We had some serious thinking to do.

Ma wanted to know who owned the Tomboy Mine. Was it a company with stockholders?

I shook my head. "Merlin told me about it. The Tomboy's a private corporation owned by the Rothschild family in Europe. They bought the mine a few years back. That's why the Tomboy has no end of capital for improvements and expansion."

"Everybody's heard of the Rothschilds," Ma said. "They have the largest fortune in the world."

"Hmm . . ." I said.

"Food for thought," Ma agreed. She was keeping her voice down. "Let's weigh one and figure out what they're worth."

"I just had one on the scale—fourteen pounds exactly." I sprang for a pencil and a scrap of cardboard. "Gold is around twenty dollars an ounce."

"Sixteen ounces to a pound," Ma said helpfully. My mother was surprising me no end. I was afraid this would tie her in knots.

"Each one is worth about four thousand five hundred dollars," I reported.

"Hmm . . . We could pay off our loan. We'd be free and clear again."

Ma's mind was racing even faster than mine. She had me wrap the gold bars in a piece of burlap and bury them on the side of the barn that couldn't be seen from the road. We were going to bide our time. Every day, we would pick up the *Durango Herald* and check for news from Telluride, looking for anything about a suspect taking a mule, anything about missing bullion. "One more thing," Ma said. "Let's keep this between us until the time's right. I can't imagine trying to think this through with Till."

"Me neither."

We waited a few days with nothing in the *Herald* and no knocks on the door. On the surface everything was quiet and peaceful, but Ma and I were on tenterhooks. "The Tomboy Mine must've known for a good while now that you took Hercules and left on the train," Ma said. "I'm wondering if they might have their own reasons for keeping it quiet and letting it go."

"I've already thought of one. They might not want to let it be known that they succeeded in making bullion."

"On top of that," Ma added with a chuckle, "they don't want to be caught looking like boneheads trying to be clever."

I figured we were of the same mind, but a couple days later, with Till off fishing, Ma up and said, "Owen, I've been thinking and praying. I don't know if we can keep the gold. I mean, if we *should* keep it. Is it righteous?"

The wind went right out of my sails. "Oh, Ma," I wailed. "What will we make in our first three years selling vegetables and strawberries? What are the chances we even break even? When that loan comes due, we'll be sunk."

"That's why I took the job, even if it was hopeless. What should we do?"

"Ma, we're under the lion's paw."

"Don't I know it."

"Think of it this way. They owe us for the use of our mule! This is what it cost them to get the core of their new compressor up the mountain. It was a lot cheaper than building a road!"

"That's a good argument, but still . . ."

Pleading, practically begging, I gave it one more try. "After all we've been through, don't we deserve a lucky break?"

A tear escaped my mother's eye as she shook her head to that. "It's a complicated moral question, Owen."

"Fine as a frog hair split three ways."

"Where'd you come up with that?"

"From Till, of course. It's from one of his 'Blood and Thunders.'"

29

WISE AS SOLOMON

A WEEK HAD gone by with nothing in the newspaper and no knocks on the door. During that time Ma heard all about our travels. It was Till who mostly filled her in on our journey with the marshal, with me trying to stay out of earshot. I happened to overhear when Till was going on about Butch and Sundance, how they'd never been caught for a robbery. Ma brought him up short and said, "Tell me what you thought of them. What were they really like?"

Till had to mull that one over. "Both got sad eyes," he said finally. I was impressed.

My time in Telluride was mostly what Ma and I talked

about. I told her about Uncle Jacob's friend, Merlin Custard. I spoke of the Smuggler-Union and the crushing defeat the miners were dealt by Colorado's high court. "In Uncle Jacob's letters," I said, "he never let on how bad the miners were up against it."

"Pa was sick, that's why," said Ma.

I gave her a detailed account of the fire and the calamity that ensued in the depths of the mine. I told her about Vincent St. John's impassioned speech at the Miners Hall, and how he asked the men to build a hospital, poor as they were.

I saved the hardest part for last. I told her that Merlin and the other men at the boarding house were convinced that Uncle Jacob had been murdered by the powers that be. Ma took that awful hard.

The day after that, with Till gone to the store for flour and eggs, Ma up and said, "Owen, how many mules would you say are at work in and around Telluride?"

"Hundreds, for sure."

"That's what I pictured. I've been doing a lot of reflection. Now tell me, what are the chances it was our Hercules carrying the bullion?"

"Mighty slim. That's what I meant by lucky break."

"Was it luck?" Ma said with a mysterious smile. "I don't think so."

"What was it, then?"

"Owen, I dreamed of your father last night. I was telling him all about it. He said don't you see, it was the

226

hand of Providence!"

"Thank you, Pa," I whispered.

"That's only part of the picture, Owen."

"How does the rest go?"

"I've been reflecting on justice in light of all that you told me about the miners. I recalled how often the subject of justice came up at the meeting house. One of those times we were discussing the word *righteousness,* in 'Blessed are they who hunger and thirst for righteousness.' We got to wondering why the word *justice* wasn't used instead."

"Come to think of it, why not?"

"It could've been, it just wasn't. We learned that it had to do with a word that could have been translated into English either way. A Greek word, I think it was. In our case, I'm thinking, the heart of the matter has more to do with justice than righteousness."

Ma looked me in the eye. I held my breath.

"One bar would be enough to keep us afloat. We would give the other one to the miners to help them build their hospital. That would give me peace. That's what Jacob would want: justice for them and justice for us. It's up to you, Owen. Only half of that gold for us, but we need to be of one mind."

"Ma," I said, "you're as wise as Solomon."

Ma wanted to wait out the rest of October before telling Till and getting in contact with Vincent St. John. We talked about taking the train to Telluride and presenting one of the ingots in person, but Ma came up with a better plan. After we figured out how to bank the gold, she would write St. John a letter and invite him to come visit in Hermosa. When he came, she would give him a check.

On the heels of our conversation, I grabbed some apples and went to see Hercules and Peaches in the pasture. I suppose it was my scientific bent, but as I fed them the apples, I was revisiting a nagging question. How was it that the Tomboy chose Hercules to carry the bullion down from the mine? Maybe the answer lies neither with luck nor Providence, I was thinking, and suddenly I had a theory. Somebody in Telluride, most likely at the stables, must have been on the lookout for a certain mule that would be easy to spot. His instructions—from Fred Tatters, most likely—were simple and went like this: *The gold will be in the panniers of that great big mule that carried the seven-hundred-pound load.*

We were anxiously counting the days as October was coming to a close without us hearing from the law. On the last day of the month, Ma spied the postman leaving something in our mailbox out on the road. As Till ran to fetch it, I thought she might faint.

On his way back, Till was holding up a single piece of mail. "Who's it for?" Ma called.

"Mary Hollowell!" he shouted. Ma and I exchanged anxious glances. Turns out it was from me, that letter from Hite City.

Ma wrote her letter to Vincent St. John that night. In

the morning she swallowed hard and let Till in on the secret. Naturally he wanted to see the gold that very minute, and was beside himself when we dug up the bars. By the time the three of us boarded the train to go to the First National Bank in Durango, Till had gotten over his injured feelings. Chalked it up to the injustice of his age and birth order, I suppose.

Cool as can be, Ma asked to see the president of the bank. We were ushered in to three chairs in front of his desk. Till knew he wasn't to say a word. I had our wicker picnic basket by my feet. Ma started in by saying she had decided to use an additional resource to pay back the loan she had recently taken out. "Happy to hear it," the banker said stuffily.

"I'll be making a deposit," Ma continued.

"Splendid, splendid."

Ma gave me a nod. I hefted our picnic basket onto his desk and lifted the cloth covering the contents. At the sight of our gold the banker said, "My, my." We held our breath as he inspected every surface without saying what he was looking for. Then he said gravely, "We'll get this asset of yours taken care of, Mrs. Hollowell. We pride ourselves on our discretion."

Before we got back on the train, Ma posted her letter to the president of Telluride's Miners Union, in which she invited Vincent St. John to visit and requested he bring Merlin Custard along if possible. Mid-November we met them at the Hermosa depot and walked them to our door. Neither knew there was more to it than a social call. Uncle Jacob had often talked about his farm, and seeing us at home in that beautiful setting made their eyes brim. When Ma presented the young leader with her check made out to the Telluride Miners Union Hospital Fund, St. John was moved and delighted. "With a gift like this," Vincent said, "we might be able to start construction in the spring."

"We're happy to hear it," Ma said.

We put them back on the train without a peep about gold bullion. If our family was to survive, the three of us must keep the secret.

30

BEFORE WE PASS ON

A WEEK AFTER Merlin and Vincent came to visit, we read
about the marshal in the *Durango Herald*. Having recently
returned from chasing a horse thief as far as Hite City on
the Colorado River, it said, Jim Clark was assassinated
on the streets of Telluride. All these years later I have
to wonder if he would've done us in. I like to think he
wouldn't have. He was gunned down shortly after midnight at the corner of Colorado and Spruce as he was
walking his nightly patrol. No suspect, no clues, only a
mention that the marshal was known to have many enemies. The marshal was buried in Telluride's Lone Tree
Cemetery. Under JAMES CLARK, his stone says CSA, for

the Confederate States of America.

Had we kept that second ingot, we could've added rooms to the house and breathed easy. As it was, we would have to keep living close to the bone. Over the next three years I gave the farm my all, trying to make it a paying proposition. Exactly one year after the fire, the new hotel and restaurant at Trimble Hot Springs had their grand opening, and Ma went back to work. She was a natural with people and loved the activity. She made the back and forth by buggy or sleigh.

As for Till, Hermosa's one-room school was a ten-minute walk from home and nothing like the chicken coop he expected. He took quite a shine to the young schoolteacher, even dropped his lingo like a hot potato for her sake. Miss Roberta introduced him to Robert Louis Stevenson and Jules Verne. Said he had "a remarkable ear for language."

Evenings those three years, I was reading and studying for the University of Colorado's entrance exams. Ma backed me all the way, but I got the idea from Molly. She entered the year before me. The university was far away in Boulder, north of Denver.

By the time I went off to college, we had five acres of vegetables and berries under cultivation. Our apple orchard of a hundred trees was coming along nicely. All three of us were keen on keeping the place. Ma gained some income by renting out the produce field and the orchard to a neighboring farmer. That left Hercules and Peaches with more than twenty acres of pasture to call their own. A couple of times a day they would get a notion and take off at a gallop. They liked to race the train and won hands down every time.

Molly and I came down from Boulder for Till's eighth-grade graduation. From Durango we went on to Telluride to see her mother. Molly's father had died the previous year, of a stroke. Her mother sold the newspaper and kept the bakery. Marie was a woman of means and loved to travel. She came twice a year to visit in Boulder.

Till went to work for a cattle rancher in the Animas Valley. He could soon throw a loop with the best of them and was wrestling steers to the ground at the age of fifteen. By eighteen the local ranch work was too tame for him. Along with a friend he'd cowboyed with in the valley, Till lit out for southeast Utah. His buddy had learned of an outfit from Texas that walked away from an enormous herd of longhorns, just abandoned them to the wilds of Cedar Mesa. Their numbers had tripled. If you had enough guts to roust them out of the canyon bottoms—Grand Gulch and Arch Canyon and all the rest—they were yours.

Till and his partner lived rough as coyotes for three or four years. It was dangerous work to say the least. Till came through it intact while his friend lost two fingers and broke some bones. They made such a hefty profit they were able to buy land and establish their own ranches.

At the university, paleontology fascinated me no end, and the same went for Molly. What could be more interesting than the history of life, with nearly all of it yet to be discovered? For our fieldwork, we had in mind a certain remote location in the San Rafael Desert. That promontory and my dinosaur tooth were anything but easy to rediscover. On my second try, with Molly on our honeymoon, I succeeded. We stacked rocks to stand on for a better look. Up close, a small portion of a second tooth was showing, and the jawbone connecting the two. We went back with photos, and they created a sensation. Nearly every professor and grad student was eager to get on board. The complete skeleton of *Ceratosaurus*, a huge predator from the Late Jurassic, was waiting for our team to tease from the rock.

Ma fell in love with a landscape painter from Vermont she met at Trimble. Once Ned saw southwest Colorado, he had a whole new world to paint, and when he discovered the canyon country with its arches, fins, natural bridges, and cliff ruins, he was head over heels. They were married in the new Friends Meeting House in Durango, and added three rooms onto the Hermosa place. Ned was a good man, and Ma found the happiness she deserved. In the '30s, during the Depression, they finally got electricity and indoor plumbing. They lived on our forty acres from Uncle Jacob until Ma passed away at the age of seventy-seven.

Till and I stayed as close as we could, given that Molly

and I were teaching at Boulder. His ranch is on Wilson Mesa, outside Telluride. It looks east at that soaring wall of mountains I tumbled down during that snowstorm in the fall of 1900. After Molly and I retired to the old place in Hermosa, I saw Till more often. It was easy to get together in the years the Rio Grande Southern was still running. We both have a passel of grandkids. Till and Beth's is the larger passel.

When our children were young, my four and Till's seven, they took our stories as factual but stretched into yarns. Their kids take them for tall tales. Till put me onto this project at a family reunion in Telluride. He said I needed to write it all down before we pass on. Not just about Butch and Sundance and the marshal and the gold, but the whole story. Start with Pa dying, Till said, and Ma having the sand to uproot herself and us and start over. And make sure to say that none of us ever got TB.

Our outlaws often come to mind. It's a wonder they were still on the loose in the first year of the twentieth century. Most of the historians believe Butch and Sundance met their end in Bolivia in 1908, at the town of San Vicente after sticking up a mine payroll. That hasn't been proved and some writers speculate that one or both lived on. Of greater interest to Till and me is the fact that they fled the United States only four months after our time with them at the Roost. It took them four months, we figure, to recover the loot they'd stashed or buried in various locations around the West. I've read a number of books about Butch Cassidy, and I chuckle at something the writers never came across: how it was that he came up with the idea of fleeing to South America.

During the time I was writing down my recollections here at Hermosa, I would often walk down the creek to a spot near its confluence with the Animas River. At the foot of the tall and solitary ponderosa where Till used to practice his knife tossing, that's where we buried H and P. The big fellow lived to the age of thirty-one, and our sweetheart to thirty-four. We nailed their marker to the tree:

HERCULES AND PEACHES
OUR FAITHFUL FRIENDS
SO FONDLY REMEMBERED

AUTHOR'S NOTE

City of Gold is a work of historical fiction. Hewing as close to history as the arc of the story would allow, I blended fact and fiction to create its characters, events, and timeline. My title jumped out at me from a 2016 publication of the Mining History Association: "Telluride's gold production (circa 1897) was so robust that the town adopted the motto 'City of Gold.'"

I set the novel in the fall of 1900, the year the photo of "The Fort Worth Five" was taken. Historians believe the photograph of the Wild Bunch had much to do with Butch Cassidy deciding to call it quits. He'd been robbing banks and trains for eleven years. Remarkably, his only prison time was eighteen months in the Wyoming pen for knowingly buying a stolen horse that cost him five dollars. Articles in *National Geographic* are thought to have played a role in his decision to flee to South America. I came across "Road to Bolivia" in the July 1900 issue of *National Geographic.*

Butch and Sundance, along with Sundance's ladylove, Etta Place, sailed out of New York Harbor on February 20, 1901, bound for Argentina. The ship was a British freighter, the

Herminius. In early March they disembarked in Buenos Aires and registered at the Europa Hotel under the name Harry A. Place, with Butch posing as Harry's brother. Butch and Sundance took along enough loot to buy a 25,000-acre ranch in Patagonia's beautiful Cholila Valley.

The Hollowells are fictional, while their Quaker background comes from the history of eastern Kansas.

Jim Clark was indeed the marshal of Telluride. He was widely believed in his time to have been complicit with Butch Cassidy in the robbery of Telluride's San Miguel Valley Bank. According to one account Clark admitted to a payoff of $2,200. Marshal Clark was assassinated in 1895. He can't object to me giving him five more years.

Bud Norton, sheriff of La Plata County, is fictional. My interest in sheriffs, marshals, outlaws, and the Wild West goes back to my childhood. William B. Rhodes, the marshal of Dodge City, Kansas, was my great-grandfather. Will Rhodes was the town marshal for ten years beginning in 1892 and later played a leading role in reinventing Boot Hill as a tourist attraction.

The Hites of Hite City, Utah, are historical. Hite City was inundated by the waters of Lake Powell, but the site reappears on the banks of the Colorado River when the reservoir recedes. The *Hoskininni* went into operation in 1901 and was abandoned the same year. The "flour gold" in the river sediment proved too fine for the dredge to collect. You have to wonder if the Navajo leader sent Cass Hite on a wild-goose chase. At the time of my story, the name "Colorado River" applied only to the river from its mouth at the Sea of Cortez up to the confluence of its two principal tributaries, the Grand River and the Green River. The Grand River was renamed the

Colorado River by a joint resolution of Congress in 1921.

Molly Dobson and her mother, Marie, are entirely fictional, but Decker Dobson (Molly's father) is based on Francis Edward Curry, the editor of Telluride's *Daily Journal* during the most contentious years in the town's history. One of Curry's rants against the miners appears verbatim in the novel. Telluride also had a weekly, the *San Miguel Examiner*. I drew heavily on its account of the Smuggler-Union disaster of November 20, 1901. In the aftermath, Local 63 charged the Smuggler-Union with criminal negligence for not having installed safety doors at the mouth of the Bullion Tunnel. Vincent St. John was the president of the local union chapter at the time, and Arthur Collins was the superintendent of the Smuggler-Union.

In 1899 the Colorado Assembly enacted the eight-hour day in mines, smelters, and blast furnaces, only to have the new law declared unconstitutional and overturned by the Colorado Supreme Court. The miners of Local 63 went out on strike on May 4, 1901. Readers might want to look into the strike and the ensuing strife that troubled Telluride through 1908. If you're looking for the hospital the miners built, you'll find the building at the northwest corner of Columbia and Pine. Opened in November 1902, it has MINERS UNION emblazoned over the portal.

Jean and I came to southwest Colorado in 1973, drawn by the shining San Juan Mountains. Early on, we rode the historic Denver and Rio Grande from Durango to Silverton, but had little sense of the former extent of Colorado's narrow gauge railroads. In years to come we drove the mountain passes with their rusty mine works on our way to the picturesque mining towns of Silverton, Ouray, and Telluride. I had more than a passing interest but only a shallow grasp of their history. When I resolved to go prospecting for a story set in their mining heyday, I had a lot to learn.

I was surprised by the extent of hard-rock mining in the San Juans—350 miles of tunnels in the Telluride area alone. The toxic legacy of the period continues to this day. In 2015, when water backed up inside a mine near Silverton and suddenly burst containment, the Animas River in Durango and the San Juan River through Shiprock ran yellow all the way to Lake Powell.

I would like to recommend the books I drew on most heavily. Richard Patterson's *Butch Cassidy: A Biography* (University of Nebraska Press, 1998) is wonderfully well researched. Brad Dimock's *The Very Hard Way: Bert Loper and the Colorado River* (Fretwater Press, 2007) includes an excellent chapter on Cass Hite and the gold flurry in Glen Canyon. Gregory Crampton's *Ghosts of Glen Canyon* (Publishers Place, 1988) has historic photos of Glen Canyon before Lake Powell, including Hite City and the Hite ferry at Dandy Crossing. When it comes to the history of the early dinosaur hunters, including Arthur Lakes, I would point you to "Science Red in Tooth and Claw," a chapter in Bill Bryson's *A Short History of Nearly Everything* (Broadway Books, 2004).

Historian Duane Smith's excellent *Song of the Hammer and Drill: The Colorado San Juans, 1860–1914* (Colorado School of Mines Press, 1982) covers the history of the mining towns, the railroads, and early Durango. Harriet Fish Backus's *Tomboy Bride* (Pruett Publishing, 1969) is rich in anecdotes of life at the Tomboy Mine, packrats and all. I am indebted to

Telluride-born historian David Lavender for *The Telluride Story* (Wayfinder Press, 2007) and his classic memoir, *One Man's West* (University of Nebraska Press, 1977), in which I learned of rustlers, running irons, and those thousands of abandoned longhorns gone wild in the canyon country.

My first glimmers of *City of Gold* came from geographer Mel Griffiths' book, *San Juan Country* (Pruett Publishing, 1984). Mel Griffiths and David Lavender both labored in Ouray's Camp Bird Mine when it reopened in the Depression. Griffiths' coverage of Telluride's mines and mills includes his accounts of the Tomboy Mine's "bullion mule" and the mule that carried the seven-hundred-pound load up to the Tomboy, both true stories.

Durango, Colorado
September 2019